PRAYING THE DAY'S NOT POISON

The Redemption of Howard Marsh 4

Bob McGough

Bearded Bard Inkworks
www.beardedbardinkworks.com

This arc of the Jubal County Saga could be called
Found Hope.
So each part is dedicated to a different group who helped
me find my Hope as an author.

To the Teachers who most influenced me:
Mrs. Rita Betts, who most embraced my writing, even
when they were just shaggy dog stories.
Dr. James Day, who taught me about Shakespearean Cir-
cles and being a cliche.
Dr. Bill Graham, for Horned Serpents and teaching me
how to think.

CONTENTS

An Introduction to Howard Marsh   IX

Pigskins   1

Find Your Legs and Go, and Stay Gone   3

Nothing to Lose   9

You Beg   16

Ramble On   19

This House Is Made of Fire   26

Like Cats and Dogs   36

So Hard to Find My Way   43

Behind the Stadium with You   52

My, How You Have Grown   57

Sometimes I'm Overcome Thinking 'Bout It   63

Smells Like Teen Spirit   68

The Goth Kid Who Won Most School Spirit   73

Lord, What Am I Doing Here?   79

Halftime, and the Living's Easy   82

We'd Finally Be Getting Down to It, but I'm an Ornery Shit   85

And Then All Hell Broke Loose   89

Mistakes Were Made   93

Nope   101

Breakers Roar   103

Down in a Hole   106

Hail Marshy   111

Touchdown   115

Bacon Wrap   121

Well That Was Anticlimactic   124

The Swamp King   129

Black Dog   131

Raise Hell, Praise Dale   142

Wheeler Dealer   152

No Good Deed   158

Sharp Pointy Teeth   164

One Lone Night   170

Time I Collect My Bones 176

I've Burned My Tongue in Thirst of Peace 185

Throwing Mud Into the Devil's Eyes 192

Just the Tip 198

Carry On, My Wayward Son 204

Dancing In the Moonlight 211

Zen the Fuck Out 218

Dreams in the Witch House 224

Should I Stay or Should I Go 230

Kiss My Ashes Goodbye 237

Burn With That Holy Ghost Fire 245

Back to Reality 250

Epilogue 253

The Back Matter! 257

Struggling with Drug Addiction? 263

An Introduction to Howard Marsh

Howard Marsh is a lot of things: a liar, a thief, a poor man's wizard. He's a shoddily tattooed skin stretched over a too skinny body that's barely held together by the same drugs that are tearing his life apart. A cynic, his words are often as poison as the substances he takes to pass his days, a suicide attempt years in the making.

He's the scion of a family with a history as rich as it is materially poor. He's the product of a miserable county with more dirt roads than paved, where poverty and loss is the order of the day. He's a man haunted by his past, and has yet to find any reason to try and piece himself back together.

You would be well advised to take what he says with a large grain of salt. He will cover the worst parts, glossing over the bits that show his darkest sides. The bits where the drugs that ravage him are in control. Where we find him is at the bottom, eking out a living as a water witch, a copper thief, a finder of lost things. Living in a storage shed and trying to maintain what's left of his frayed relationships with the few family members who will still talk to him.

But dear readers, he's a better man than he thinks. He doesn't see it; he's long forgotten the possibility even, and no one left in his life sees it either. But, if you can endure the miserable existence of watching someone make nothing but bad choices for a time, then you will perhaps be rewarded. Maybe you will see him slowly scrabble out of the muddy, trash filled ditch that is his life.

It won't be quick, and it won't be painless. The stories to come are often filled with sadness. The fairytale ending is not for stories such as these. There is a chance at happiness, but it is a long way away, and there are many obstacles both in him, and in his path.

This is not a plea for understanding, or forgiveness, or any sort of justification. It is just the way of things.

He is Howard Marsh, the Methgician.

And he doesn't give a damn what you think.

PIGSKINS

Being the Seventh Tale in the Redemption of Howard Marsh

Find Your Legs and Go, and Stay Gone

Normally I would have told Winston Summerall to burn in hell, and to shove his football somewhere mighty uncomfortable. But, seeing as it was a Saturday afternoon and I somehow didn't have a hangover, I was feeling generous.

To wind things back ever so slightly, Friday nights were always the big party night for me and Anna. We both had some steam to blow off usually—her from school, me from avoiding work like the plague—so we had a standing Friday appointment to tie one on good and proper. By the time Saturday rolled around, we'd both usually be pretty hungover. Hell, sometimes we'd still be straight up drunk, if the night had gotten real wild.

But next week was finals, so Anna had been keeping her head in a book all weekend. Which cut into our party time, sure. But . . . I don't know. It had been kinda nice, I guess. Since fall was coming on good and proper now, it wasn't balls hot in my shed, so it actually felt pretty pleasant.

So that Saturday Anna was sitting there on my foldout couch, a half dozen books and notepads laid out in a half circle around her, using a highlighter for its intended purpose, which was admittedly rare in the Marsh domicile—at least if I had I been left to my own devices. We both had a good high going thanks to some killer weed she'd gotten from her dealer up in the Gump, and I was kicked back in my broken recliner reading this shitty little sci-fi book I'd stolen from the Christian Mission donation box.

It was trash, but I was high enough that it didn't really matter. My little box fan was humming along, and we had a little music going. It played ever so faintly so as not to take us out of what we was doin' but just enough to soothe the soul, you know? Fuck, it was nice.

So when I heard the crunch of tires on gravel, I just assumed it was someone coming to use the U-Store-It for its intended purpose: to hold their junk. I did not expect to see a brand-spanking-new brilliantly white truck pull up about twenty feet from the front of my shed. And I mean that sucker was fancy, with a capital *F*. Fancy.

You see, I don't know how it is in the bigger cities, but out here in the more rural areas and small towns, rich folks don't normally have storage units. Why would they? They usually just bought or built their own outbuilding or barn to hold all their extra shit. Which really was a pisser, since I would have relished cracking open some rich folk storage units sometime, instead of just finding some old guy's porn stash he was hiding away from his wife and kids.

So the truck surprised me enough to cause me to sit up a bit and cast an eye over at Anna. She was watching the truck, too, her highlighter in one hand, a smoke in the other. She didn't have on pants, but her shirt was long enough that it had her decent enough for company. Leastways she wasn't racing to cover up.

But then the asshole to end all assholes stepped out the truck, and I just leaned back and swore under my breath.

"Who's that?" Anna asked, low enough that the man couldn't hear.

"Fucking Summerall," I spat.

"Who?"

"The car dealer guy from Sumpville."

"Oh. Ew," she said, pulling out a blanket to cover her legs.

"Ew" was right. Winston Summerall had been a quarterback for the Sumpville Lions back in the early nineties. He was that sort of preppy fuck that should have been off at the county private school, since his folks were the closest thing to Sumpville royalty, but I think they knew what a little shit he was and were trying to try and choke a little humility down his throat. It didn't take, though, seeing as he was damn near God's gift to the game of football in a county plumb mad for it. Took Sumpville to the state championships, twice, and even won one of 'em.

As little as I gave a fuck about football, even I knew that. The man was a legend, basically, and there wasn't a soul in Sumpville that was going to let us provincials out in Elk Grove forget it.

The guy was even good enough to get a free ride to Bama. He could have made it to the pros, most folks said. But pieces of shit are gonna piece of shit, and he blew his chance by partying right out. Like, partying so hard that even the scummiest of underhanded tactics by the coaches couldn't keep him on board. I think he went to some junior college for a year or two after that, some place where Daddy's money went a little farther, but I guess it didn't matter too much in the end.

At some point he took over the family car dealership, and as usually happens—because God doesn't pay us any attention anymore—it started doing fan-fucking-tastic. Maybe it was that tangential connection to playing for

Gene Stallings, no matter how briefly. But to say Winston Summerall was rich was like saying I sometimes dabbled in intoxicants; while true, it didn't quite paint the full picture. Fucker was *loaded.*

Out he stepped from that too-nice truck, sporting snake-skin cowboy boots and an honest-to-god Stetson that he had to put on when he got out because it was too tall for him to wear inside the cab. It was like if Don Johnson and a cowboy had a love child with too many perfect teeth and too much fake tanner.

He did have some damn nice teeth, though. And seeing as he didn't once stop smiling that greasy car salesman smile from the moment he left the cab, I had plenty of time to marvel. Then he reached back inside the cab, leaning over the center console, and scooped up a football. Damn thing was branded with the Sumpville Lions logo. And that was the moment I knew that everything that was about to happen was probably going to be real fucking dumb. Nothing makes folks more stupid in the county than football.

"Mr. Marsh!" Summerall said casually as he walked toward my shed, idly tossing that football back and forth between his hands. I think he did it mostly to make the state champ ring he wore glint in the sunlight. Because, of course, he still wore it proudly. "Fine day out today, don'tcha think?"

He was disgustingly perfect. Smooth, friendly voice, too-nice teeth, dashing good looks. Fuck, he made me sick. But . . . it was a nice day. And I wasn't hungover. So, I decided to make an honest effort, since Anna was there. "Yeah, though I ain't exactly been out in it."

He stood in the opening to my shed, there beneath the roll-up door, and I saw his eyes quickly glance around. If my chaos bothered him, he didn't show it. "Fair enough," he chuckled. He nodded over to Anna and, no shit, tipped his hat. "Afternoon, ma'am."

"Afternoon," she mumbled, going back to her books. She was making it clear that none of this concerned her, that she had more important things to tackle, which I think was mostly directed at me.

I ain't a total idiot. I can take a hint.

And hell, sometimes I even listen to them.

Nothing to Lose

I stood up, grunting a little as I straightened my back. My broken chair was comfortable enough, but it had a way of contorting my back if I sat in it too long. "Now's as good a time as any to get out in it, I reckon. Let's step outside so she can study."

Summerall stepped out of the doorway and back out into the light and I joined him, fishing out a cigarette from the almost empty pack in my pocket.

"I appreciate you giving me a bit of your time, Mr. Marsh. I'd actually stopped by your grandmother's place first. I swear, I've been going out there for years now, and she hasn't aged a day! Good genes there!"

The fact that he would just pop on over to Granny's said a lot about why his business was probably doing as well as it was. Nothing else in the county was doing half as good these days, it seemed. "Something like that," I said around the cigarette as I lit it.

"She was a touch busy, though, she said, so she sent me to see your cousin. Krista, I think's her name. Pretty girl . . . maybe a smidge less friendly, though?"

That drew a laugh from me. Granny was dead set on Krista being her heir, and Krista basically just wanted to set Granny on fire most days. So it was good to know that Krista wasn't gonna play the old bitch's games. "She's a bit touchy, yeah."

That damn smile never faltered. "She was, at that. She told me that if I wanted some help that my best bet would be looking you up. So, here I am! I have to admit, I've done a fair bit more driving today than I thought I would, and seen a good bit more of your family than I would have imagined."

"And just what sort of problem is bad enough to drag you out of Sumpville?" It was fucking bright out, and while in the shade of my shed the heat felt ok, it was actually a bit much without sunglasses. I wanted this conversation over, quick, so I could go back to where it was cool and dark.

"The obvious, of course," he said, as though I had any sort of clue what he was talking about.

I just stared at him blankly. I was being nice, but I had a real firm limit on how nice I was prepared to be, and talking at that exact second would probably have had me toeing the line.

"The season." The same expectant tone.

I stared back, a little less blankly, a little more angrily.

For the very first time, that smile faltered as the faintest hint of confusion entered the field. "Football, Mr. Marsh. The Lions' season this year . . . ? Haven't you been paying attention?"

I should have known. I couldn't help rolling my eyes. "I'm not much for the high school stuff."

I might as well have kicked the man's puppy.

"Oh man, Mr. Marsh . . . you are missing out. High school ball is where the real passion is! Kids playing for the pure love of the game, a community coming together! It's . . . it's . . . magical!" He gave a sort of awkward glance around when he said "magical." It was like he was saying something shameful, or something he shouldn't say in front of me, which made it real clear that he was seeing me to deal with something like that. I guess that should have been clear from him going to Granny, then Krista, then me as a last resort, but it was nice to have confirmation.

"Well, seeing as I'm a bit past playing age, what does it have to do with me?"

"Cheating," Summerall snarled, as though it was an actual curse word.

"You tryna hire me to help you cheat, or to catch some cheaters?" I didn't really care one way or the other, honestly, if the money was right and no one was gonna get hurt.

That wounded look returned, wiping the anger right off the man's face. "What? God, no. I mean, yes, catch some cheaters, but we don't need to *cheat*!"

"We" being the Lions, of course, and I was slowly figuring out that Summerall must be some sort of booster for the team. Which made sense; I just didn't ever pay attention to shit like that. In Elk Grove, it was real popular to hate the Lions since they pretty much beat our local Elks handily each year, but I doubt the Lions really paid us any mind. You can't really work up a hate for a team you pity, I reckon, so the rivalry was really just one-sided.

"Who's cheatin', then?"

The car dealer's eyes narrowed. "The Swampcats."

The team of the only other public school in the county, and the smallest at that. Burgamy Village was way down south in Jubal County, right on the edge, and I never tended to make it down that way. Elk Grove was a backwater, sure, but fuck me if Burgamy Village wasn't even worse.

Bay Houdan was about the only place more backwards, and that place was just about dead.

"So they're cheating. How?" I wasn't about to take Winston Summerall, of all people, at face value.

The man's knuckles started to whiten where his hand was clamped onto that football. He was gripping it so hard I thought he might pop the damn thing. "They have twenty-one guys on their team—that's it. Some of those guys are having to Ironman it. But they're undefeated, and it's not even been close! There's no way they can be that good and keep beating bigger teams like they are. Have you seen the scores? They usually win by at least twenty, even against teams that are otherwise undefeated! There's no way they aren't cheating. And it's not with the refs; I made sure of that."

I didn't bother to ask how he knew there was no bribery going on. Rich folks, I reckon, know a lot more about bribery than me. One of the pros of actually having money, I suppose. But it also made me think . . .

Summerall was putting on a damn good show about hating cheating. But add in what I knew about him, and what I knew about how big-name boosters tended to act, and the fact he knew how to check on the bribing of a ref to such a surety, well . . . two and two and two made six. And in this case, six smelled like a cheater to me. He came across real friendly and on the level, but . . . well, not to be super cliché, but he *was* a car salesman.

Sometimes things are cliché for a reason.

"So you think they're getting magic help somehow. You got any proof?"

He at least had the decency to look a little sheepish at that question. "Not exactly. Like, nothing I can point to directly. But that would be the point, right? If it was blatant, everyone would know! But you see, most folks don't know about . . . what *we* know about. Right? So they don't know what to look for. But I'm telling you, if you go to the game this Friday, you'll be able to tell."

"So, to be clear, you want to hire me to stop whatever magic is helping them."

"Right. And you have to have it done before the Lions play them. Which isn't this Friday, or the next, but the Friday after that. Find who or what is helping them, and stop it. Should be pretty easy for someone of your talents."

That drew a laugh. "Clearly you don't have my kinda luck if you think that. So, let's talk pay . . ."

I managed to talk him up to two hundred up front to cover expenses, which would be turned into drugs, most likely. And then if the Lions beat the Swampcats, I would get a further eight hundred. Now that had the potential to get me caught up on rent for a change.

I could live with that.

He threw in the football for free, but as soon as he was gone I chucked it into the DQ dumpster. Made it on the first try too. Maybe I should have been a quarterback.

You Beg

Now, I could have been proactive. I could have gone out the moment Summerall left and started beatin' the bushes, trying to catch wind of what was going on. I could have at least trekked down to Burgamy Village to check out the lay of the land.

But that would have taken work. And effort. So, I didn't do any of those things.

Instead, I did a lot of drugs. I mean, I had to catch up from the weekend study-palooza and all! Standards have to be maintained and all that. So that meant catching a ride out to Jimmy's, and then that of course turned into a two-day stay in his camper, where there was no sleep to be had thanks to a staggeringly good cook he had just finished.

That led to a brief interlude where I got lost as hell in the woods behind his camper for about seven hours on a bad acid trip. That left me kinda stove up, seeing as

I fell down into a gully at some point and landed in a briar patch, which wasn't a great move. Tripping literally while tripping mentally is never a good combo, and it left me with a badly sprained shoulder and ankle. Damn near broke my collarbone, too, I think.

I was lucky that Jimmy found me or hell, some coyotes or such might have eaten me. Not that it would be the first time a coyote had tried to eat me . . . but I didn't think I would be so lucky the second time.

The moral of that story should be "Drugs are bad," but I chose to go with "Fuck nature."

By the time Friday rolled around, I was in that "damn near too stiff to move" phase of healing. In a fit of wounded pride, I hadn't told Anna about my . . . adventure, so when she showed up to my shed about six o'clock, she was big mad. *Big* mad.

And you know, I could have just taken it on the chin. But sometimes the devil just gets in me, and I can't just let things be. So she took to yelling—from a good place, a worried place. The kind of yelling that was all filled with tears, because she loved me and she didn't want me to die. Which, let's be real, was a legitimate risk at the rate in which I partook, not even factoring in potential falls into gullies.

But among my many flaws is a perverse streak of pride. It's totally undeserved, but it's there, and the words she hurled my way kicked my scruff up in a big way. So, I took to shoutin' back. Things got a little heated, to put it lightly. I thought she was gonna slap me at one point—which, seeing as Anna wouldn't hurt a fly under normal circumstances, should tell you about how pissed I got her.

She left around six fifteen.

That's when my pride deflated and I realized I had fucked up. I tried calling her a half dozen times and she didn't answer, not that I blame her. We'd fought before, of course; any couple that doesn't get at least a little snippy with each other just plumb isn't invested enough in each other, I figure. But this was by far the worst, and I felt pretty damn terrible.

So what does all this have to do with the price of tea in China, as my uncle HD would say?

It meant that by the time I finally got on the road to Burgamy Village, the game had already been well started, and I was both physically and mentally a bit of a wreck. Maybe more than a bit.

Things were off to a great start.

Ramble On

So for those not from the county, what you need to realize is that Elk Grove is at the top, more or less. Then there's Sumpville around the middle, and in the far southeast is Burgamy Village. Being in the north part of the county, most times it was just easier to head up to Montgomery to get anything Elk Grove didn't have to offer—which was basically everything worth a damn.

That all said, I didn't really make it down to Sumpville all that often, unless it was to go to court. Being the county seat, a lot of the overhead of being me came from visits down there to try and weasel out of fines or fight to stop from getting pinged for some sort of parole violation. I mean, it never worked in my favor—at least not without a little magical aid—but a boy has to try, you know?

Being as the courthouse was only open in the day, it had been some years since I had ridden through Sumpville at night. To be honest, it did the town a lot of favors. It might have been the county seat, and where the most money was, but that didn't mean there was anywhere near enough to go around. It was just as shitty as the rest of Jubal County, only it tried to pretend otherwise.

I was riding with Liam in his new Civic. The past year had been pretty good to him, at least. He'd gotten himself a good job as a mechanic at a dealership up in Montgomery, and his girlfriend, Marketta, was now his fiancé. I'd helped a tiny bit with the first part of that, using a little of my hoodoo to find out just how much they would be willing to go up to on pay, and so he owed me a favor.

With Anna not answering my calls and me needing a ride to the game, it was time to cash it in, I reckoned. And fuck me if he wasn't a good sort and came around quick as you please. Actually, that sort of fueled my feeling like shit; I didn't deserve a friend that good.

I suppose Liam could tell that I didn't feel much like talking. He gave me a beer, and I sipped it slowly as we passed down the highway that split Sumpville right down the middle. Follow it far enough and we'd hit the beach. I wondered what that would be like.

For a moment, I just wanted to chuck it all away and ask him to just keep driving. He could leave me at the beach, and I'd figure things out. Not like I had anything worth trying to keep here. If Anna was done with me . . .

I stared out the window, trying my best not to draw attention to the couple of tears that had flowed on out. I wanted to just open the car door and go rolling out into traffic. I'd fucked up, again, and I was tired of fucking up.

I was fucking tired, down to my soul.

I couldn't help but think of Jerm. He was a shit, but I missed him.

I missed a lot of folks. Too many people in my life were dead now, and here I was, alive, in spite of my best efforts. It damn sure wasn't fair.

To say I didn't want to do this job was a woeful understatement. But it wasn't like I had anything else to do now. And if I was busy, maybe I wouldn't keep checking my phone every two minutes, seeing if I had missed a call or text.

A glow began to fill the horizon to my right. As we passed through town, the light got brighter and brighter till it blotted out all the stars. Only the partial moon could be seen, and it looked pale by comparison. "Is that the stadium?" I asked.

Liam glanced to the right. "Yeah. Must be a home game tonight."

"Fuck, that's bright."

"I don't guess you've seen it, but they've sunk a lot of money into that place over the last couple years. Like, over a million, easy, I bet."

"A million fucking dollars on a small-town football stadium? Bullshit."

"Your boy did it."

I snorted. He knew, in the loosest of terms, what had me out and about. "Summerall? He paid for it? Bullshit. He's rich, but he ain't *that* fucking rich."

Liam shrugged. "Not all of it, but he, like, what do they call it . . . matched? Yeah, he matched what other folks raised. It might not be a million, but it's still a hell of a lot of money."

I looked at the clock on his dash. We had time. I mean, we was already late; what was a few more minutes? "Drive me by it real quick. I wanna see."

I wish I hadn't asked.

The stadium was behind the school, so we had to go around to get to it. And though I hadn't been over there in about a decade, I guessed, it looked almost fucking identical. They might have sunk a million dollars into the stadium, but other than what looked like a couple of trailers off to one side, I couldn't see where any of those dollars had gone into the school itself.

It was the same redbrick buildings with gray roofs and white trim. The paint had been kept up, at least, but even in the dark I could tell the few roofs I could see needed some love. The gym was still the same ratty-looking steel building it had always been, making it clear that basketball didn't get any love either. That's Alabama for you, though. If it ain't football, it can fuck off, in most people's opinion.

As we turned the corner and started going around the side of the block, you could see the stadium more or less clearly for the first time. He was right; they had sunk some serious money into it. The scoreboard was new, and it had a damn TV in it! It wasn't mega huge, and looked like it was just playing ads for local sponsors, but it was a TV nevertheless. The press box was, say, three stories high now, and had the stadium not been on a lower level than the school, it would have been taller even than the gym.

But the stands were where the most money went. Even the visitor side, which used to be just a couple of rows of portable stands, had gotten some attention. I bet it could have held a few thousand folks, though to be fair I'm really shit at guessing numbers.

As it was, there were a fuck-off lot of people there. The parking lot was full, and cars lined all the streets. A few of the closer houses had turned into small lots with paid parking for those folks too lazy to walk too far. I couldn't really blame them. To hell with football games, and that goes double for ones you gotta walk to.

We weren't the only cars creeping by. In fact, we were just one of a small convoy. Folks too cheap to buy a ticket but who still wanted to keep up with the game would do these slow passes by so they could see the score and catch a glimpse of the game. They had done it back when I was in school, too, but I seemed to recall more folks doing it back then. I guess the price of gas made buying a ticket more appealing.

My brief glimpse of the inside of the stadium was a riot of blue and green. The field, of course, was green, but so were the uniforms of the other guys. Green helmets, green socks, all that sort of shit. I hadn't a clue who they were, and my vision was such that I couldn't see anything that would clue me in. The blue belonged to the uniforms of the home team and several hundred fans sitting up in the stands. Even the press box was painted blue, with a big-ass white lion head featured on the front.

Something big must have happened, because right about the time we were turning the corner to head on, a roar erupted in the stands. Folks were jumping to their feet, just really going nuts. But, like I said, we were turned too far away to see what it was, and frankly I just didn't have a fuck to give. The score had been all tied up when I last saw the scoreboard, so maybe someone had broken it. I hoped it was the green nobodies, because fuck Sumpville.

The shouts lingered on in our ears for a bit, but we had places to be.

Burgamy Village awaited.

This House Is Made of Fire

Highway 346 ran through right down the middle of Burgamy Village, a two-lane stretch that, if you followed it long enough, would take you to the beach. But the highway was four lanes on either side of the town, which made it a natural bottleneck every summer. That was the only thing that kept the town alive, as near as I could tell. Folks hangry from the slow-moving traffic deciding to stop at the half dozen gas stations and restaurants, usually in a failed attempt to wait out the worst of it, were the main source of income.

As the road narrowed to two lanes, we passed a few houses and the first couple gas stations. Even though it was late, more than a few of the houses had no windows of light peeking out. The houses loomed there just off the road, squat shapes that probably looked better in the dark—a lot like me, I reckon.

The gas stations were better lit, of course, and it was there that you could see the bulk of folks who, like me, were a little bit social but didn't give a rip about football. A bevy of jacked-up trucks loomed large, most of them endowed a smattering of gun racks and rebel flags. November's deer season was an eternity away for folks like that, so they tended to congregate in small clumps while they gassed up and bought beer, prepping for a night spent mudding and riding dirt roads.

A couple of restaurants were up and running. The Hardees looked especially dingy and empty, but Janice's Shack looked like it was passably busy. I saw a few others, but one was boarded slap up, and the other two must have only offered lunch or something, 'cause they were totally dead except for the odd security light.

And that was basically the sum total of nightlife in Burgamy Village. I thought Elk Grove was a miserable shithole, but damned if the Village wasn't somehow even worse. And fuck if it wasn't dark; it also seemed to be lacking most lights a normal town would have. I guess most folks were too poor to pay to keep security lights running, and there didn't seem to be much in the way of any city lighting. The whole place felt like the set of some low-budget horror movie or something. I half expected us to see some blood-covered topless co-ed come running out into the street, axe murderer a few steps behind her.

That would have actually been interesting, though, so of course it didn't happen.

We did see one nice big suburban SUV painted up in cop colors, parked right where the speed limit dropped to thirty-five. Liam weren't no fool, though, and he'd slowed down well before rounding that curve. My butthole may have puckered a bit as my mind immediately went to the drugs I had on me, but thankfully we passed on without so much as a flicker of lights.

The city was basically one giant speed trap, so once it dropped to thirty-five, we had about another quarter mile before it dropped to twenty-five. That was where the school sat. It was situated smack in the middle of town and right off the highway, but still, it wasn't even a quarter as brightly lit as the school we had just left a bit ago.

Parking was also not nearly the issue it was up in Sumpville, as Liam fairly quickly proved by parking on the side of one of the little side roads that circled the campus. We were at the tail end of a line of cars, and Liam's was definitely one of the nicer ones that I could see. It was almost heartwarming to know that the blight that was Jubal County descended this far south. Sumpville actually had a little money—for football, at least. Burgamy Village struck me more as the kind of place that may have heard of "money" once in passing but had no real personal experience with it. It certainly appeared that way, anyway.

We sat there in the car for a few minutes, finishing our cigarettes and pounding a beer each. Unless things were dramatically different than when I had last been in school, there was no smoking or drinking permitted on the premises, and there was no way I was gonna go in there with my head on fully straight. I'd have smoked a joint, too, if I wasn't scared of some parent getting their undies in a bunch because they smelled weed. Last thing I needed was some security officer or cop harassing me.

"Do you miss it?" Liam asked in between drags on his cigarette.

"Miss what? School?" I laughed. "Fuck no. I hated it bad enough back then that I didn't finish, and I ain't had any mind to ever try and go back."

"I meant the games," he responded, pointing off toward the lights of the game going on a couple hundred feet away.

"Never got the point. Why the hell does a broke-ass school system sink money into something like sports?"

Liam shrugged and finished his beer. I polished mine off a couple of seconds later, and with that we finally climbed out the car. I flicked my smoke through the chain-link fence onto the school grounds. It was petty, but then I was feeling petty. I was in a mood, that was for sure, and if I was being honest with myself, I wasn't really fit for being around folks just then. I could feel my ornery streak flaring up, and that usually meant self-inflicted trouble was coming.

I needed to get away from Liam before I worked myself out from a ride home.

The school itself was much like every other school in the county: brick, old, and not in the best shape. Honestly, the repetition was getting old and boring even to me, and I was the one living it. The only difference between here and Sumpville that I could see from the road was that there were fewer buildings, and the gym was not as tall. Oh, and there was a lot of orange.

Which made sense, seeing as the school color for the Swampcats was orange. I didn't think that made a lot of sense personally, but then what the hell even is a swampcat? I mean, I knew what Burgamy Village called a swampcat, and near as I could tell it was some sort of panther.

You'll understand if I am a bit skittish around panthers these days.

As we walked alongside the school grounds toward the field, I could hear the staticky mumbling of the guy calling the game over ancient tinny speakers. There were also the sounds of whistles, pads colliding—the usual football sounds. I hadn't been to a football game in at least a decade, but the sounds and smells were trickling in, tickling that little part of your brain that says "Hey, this is familiar."

The football field was a square of light in the otherwise dark town. It was bright, *real* bright, even with about one bulb in four blown out or missing, from the looks of things. Those remaining lights didn't do the area any favors either. No money had been sunk here like back up in Sumpville. In fact, I couldn't see anything that looked like it might have been built in this century.

The home side stands were well-worn aluminum stands five rows high. They lined about forty yards of the field at the bottom of a low slope that reached up to touch what looked like the cafeteria and a playground. The far side, the visitor side, didn't even have stands, instead boasting a long set of wooden benches with no backs, like the world's shittiest church pews. I wasn't surprised to see no one was using them, the few visiting parents and such opting to sit on folding chairs they'd brought instead. All thirty or so of them.

While the school was surrounded by a low chain-link fence, the field was left open. So really, there was nothing to stop us from just walking in if we wanted, aside from some sad-sack cop or something that might stop us. Either way, we made our way over to a table that had been set up where a couple of older women were taking money for tickets inside. Since it was almost halftime, there wasn't exactly a line; in fact, we were the only ones walking up.

A woman with denture-perfect teeth smiled at me as we approached. "Five each, please," she beamed at us. The other lady was . . . less friendly. She sorta glared at me, which was a pretty clear indication she had a good idea who I was. But as I didn't know her from Jesus, I just tried to ignore her.

I made no move to pay, in hopes that Liam would spring for the tickets. But he just stood there, looking out at the game, not paying me or the ladies any attention. So, begrudgingly, I rooted around in my pocket to pull out a wrinkled ball of bills. I set it out on the table and started to pull dollar bills from the ball one at a time, making a big show of straightening them out as I went.

Now I did have a ten in my wallet, but I had learned that sometimes folks would get so annoyed with waiting on you to dig out the exact change that they would just give up and make up the difference. So, I stood there and nonchalantly worked that ball into a crinkly stack of eight dollars. Then I began to pat my other pockets, like I was trying to find the rest of what I needed.

It *almost* worked. That smiling woman started to reach for my eight ones, and I even heard her start to say, "Well, it's almost half time anyway . . ."

Then Grumpy Pants beside her, glaring at me all the while, reached out and placed a hand on the nice woman's arm, stopping her. She didn't say anything, but it was pretty clear who the boss was in this little duo. Nice Lady pulled her hand back, giving me a sort of "nothing I can do" smile/shrug combo.

I wouldn't have been pissed, except that my little scheme had almost worked. So even though I still had the ten, I made a point to pay in the assortment of pennies, nickels, and a quarter that I had in my pocket. I wanted to huff up a storm, and in fact I had to really fight to keep from having a little snit fit, but fuck if I was going to give that grump the satisfaction. It was enough to make me wish I had something petty, like a shoelace curse so her shoes wouldn't stay tied.

Instead, I had to settle for taking my two hard-earned tickets and handing one to a still-oblivious Liam. He took it without a word of thanks, the ungrateful bastard, and set off for the stands. He was waving at someone, so I guess he knew folks down this way. I saw who was waving back—some old white guy in a green blazer, of all things—and knew I wanted no part of that. So, I decided to stick to my plan of getting away from Liam for a bit and seeing if I could manage to shake this mood of mine.

The smell of shitty ballgame food was filling my nose, and even though I wasn't all that hungry, I figured I would at least go and see what the food situation was like. I kinda wanted popcorn, but that wasn't really an option with teeth like mine. But I knew that if I waited too long it would be halftime, and that's when every jackoff in the place would be in line. With a new determination, I started following my nose in the direction of the concessions.

The press box, where I gathered the concession stand was located, bore a sign that read Ward Peebles Stadium. It also had one of those derpy panthers plastered across the side of it, just like how Sumpville had a lion on theirs. That was the only thing that looked like it had seen a fresh coat of paint in the past few years, as it was only a little faded and the paint hadn't begun to flake away. The same could not be said for the scoreboard, half of which didn't seem to even be able to light up.

To my left I could see the back of a bunch of sets of legs through the gaps in the stands. There was clearly a good crowd out, but I reckon winning will do that. I imagined those same stands had been a lot emptier this time last year.

There were a few kids playing under the stands, doing whatever it is little kids who don't give a damn about football do. I didn't pay them much mind, other than to step around one annoying little shit who just about ran smack into me. He took a tumble and face-planted right as I did it, which no doubt made it look like I had tripped him or something. He started to squall, of course, but thankfully no adults were paying any attention. I was here for a reason, and that reason wasn't to be kicked out.

I could have helped him up, but, well, he probably should have been watching where he was going better. Plus, I ain't much of one for kids. I don't particularly care to be around them in the best of times, and this was far from the best of times. Him emitting a sound not unlike a tiny tornado siren didn't exactly endear him to me, either.

Kid left in the dirt, I made my way to the concession stand.

Suddenly I wanted a hot dog real bad.

Like Cats and Dogs

The hot dog was not even barely passable.

Now while I typically go as cheap as possible in all things—stolen or free, preferably—there are two things I will spend more than the minimum on. First, of course, are drugs. I will spend money I don't have every day and twice on Sunday for drugs.

The second are hot dogs. If it's not an all-beef frank, you can not-so-kindly fuck right off.

This, my friends, was not an all-beef frank.

As my dad would have said, had he been there, it was "all just peckers and lips." The man is a demon made flesh, but he has a way with words sometimes, and he's not wrong. This was clearly made from the bottom of the random meat barrel, and to make it even worse, I had just paid a small-town stadium price for it.

Four dollars—*four dollars* to suffer through this atrocity of a dog. I wanted to toss it, it was such a disappointment. If I was a hot dog, this would be me, just chock full of bad chemicals, cancer-causing agents, and failure. And the bun was so stale that it could probably have withstood gale force winds before bending. I didn't even bother trying to mask it all with ketchup. I had no doubt that if I had tried that, as soon as I went to squeeze out the ketchup, all that would have come out was watery tomato.

I almost threw it at that stumbling kid making his snotty-faced way in my general direction, no doubt on a quest for his mom. But instead, I just tossed it into the trash and decided to feel real bad about myself.

This Anna thing was really getting to me, I reckoned.

I needed to distract myself before I caused a ruckus, and actually doing what I had come here to do seemed to be my best bet. So, four dollars lighter and a whole lot of disappointment heavier, I decided to make my way into the stands. I needed to see the lay of the land and start trying to figure out if anything magic was going on.

It's one thing to see the back of a bunch of legs and another entirely to see the rest of all those orange-clad folks. There was a broad swathe of folks filling those stands, and all in all it looked like a goddamn pumpkin patch run amok. I like Halloween, but if I'm being honest, orange is a really god-awful color. It was quite a sight. At least it wasn't the same pumpkin-puke Tennessee orange, else I might have just said "fuck it" and left.

I spotted Liam off down on the far end talking to a small clump of people, so I decided it might be best to keep to this end. If I ended up doing something stupid, I didn't want him to be caught up in my bullshit. So I started eyeing around for a good spot that wasn't too crowded, some place where I would have a little elbow room.

What I found instead was fucking Morgan. Worse, she saw me too.

If she hadn't spotted me, I think I would have just said "Fuck Summerall!" and convinced Liam that we had to get. But that ship sailed as soon as she damn near jumped to her feet and started over toward me. She was grinning like a possum eatin' briars, and I was absolutely certain that didn't bode well for me. I actually turned to start walking off, but all that did was show me that there was no place close enough for me to hide. There was the press box, and out past that, far enough, were some trees where I could see a couple of folks flitting around the edge of the light. Both were too far for me to escape to before she could get to me.

That said, what we would likely need to say would best not be heard by the locals, I reckoned, so I did walk away a bit over to one of the trash cans. I saw my forlorn wannabe hot dog sitting on top of the trash, and it seemed like an apt metaphor for how my night was going. I kinda wanted to join it in there.

"Howard," Morgan crooned as she drew close. She was one of the few not dressed in orange, but she still looked off somehow. She was dressed like some sort of terrible cliché movie take on a tarot card reader, all scarves and flowy clothes. They didn't look warm, but I knew good and well that she could use her magic to keep her warm if it got too cold.

I wished I could do that. Krista had made mutterings about showing me, but getting her to teach me anything was like pulling teeth more often than not.

"Morgan. Didn't reckon on seeing you here."

She laughed. "Not as much as it's a surprise to see you. I didn't think the old bitch would let you come this far south."

I had no idea what she was talking about, other than the fact she was referring to Granny, no doubt. I decided that letting her know that was probably not in my best interest. I set a goal for getting out of this conversation with her learning as little as possible, and I would just ask HD later what she meant. "Well, you know how it is," I answered with a shrug.

She eyed me—at least I thought she did. Her face was a little shadowed where we were standing, which I was sure meant my face was lit as hell for her perusal. *Fuck.*

"Why are you here, Howard? Is it because of me?" She was bristling up like a porcupine.

"Nope. What's going on between you and Granny, that's between you two," I said, hoping she could tell just how truthful I was being. I doubted she would make a move on me with all these people around, but that's the thing about a briar witch: the older they get, the more insane they become.

"Hmmm." Her tone was distrustful. "Again, why are you here? You know you aren't meant to be any farther south than Grady Ferry."

Grady Ferry had been a little village once, but these days it wasn't even a spot on the map. It was just a volunteer fire department and a gas station about five miles north of Burgamy Village. I didn't know, but judging from the fact that there was a bridge there, I reckoned there had been a ferry once. My lack of local history knowledge aside, I still had no clue what she was on about. I mean, yeah, I'd only ever really passed through these parts, never lingered—but I hadn't known I wasn't *allowed.*

If I wasn't allowed, and Morgan knew about it, then no doubt it had to do with some magic bullshit. Probably some really crucial bit of information Granny had never relayed to me.

"Just here to see the game. Heard they're doing big things down this way." She had no idea that I didn't give a shit about high school football. In fact, being from the county, it would make even more sense for me to be a fan. Not giving a fuck made me a bit of an outlier.

"I call bullshit. If you're violating the Ban, then it's for more than to see some heads smack."

I wanted to smack Granny with everything I had for keeping me so blind. "Believe what you want. Now I got a game to watch," I said, moving to walk around her.

Her hand snaked out, and she grabbed my arm. I could feel the power welling up in her, and I saw lightning in her eyes. She was about to fry my ass. I started calling up power of my own, but I knew I was going to be too late.

Then she shoved me away and wheeled so that she was no longer facing me. I felt the power still welled up inside her, but it wasn't lashing out. Instead, she spat a few words at me. "Go on, then."

I could hear her breathing heavy and her whole body was sorta heaving, as if she was fighting a war inside herself. Honestly, she probably was. Briar witches are called that because of how the magic just rips and tears at their minds, and given long enough, they all eventually go insane. And I knew Morgan was pretty well along down that path.

I'd have felt pretty bad for her if she hadn't kidnapped me—and, you know, just probably thought real hard about killing me. So I took my chance and just stalked on, hoping I wouldn't just burst into flames or something.

Fuck, it was terrifying. I kept calling up my power, ready to try and defend myself, and hauled ass back to the front of the stands where I was more fully in view of the assembled masses. I guessed that I was doing a pretty good job of hiding just how scared I was, because the few people who glanced my way left them at that: just glances. No one gave me so much as another look, the game absorbing all their attention.

Crazy how danger can be all around you and you might never even realize it.

So Hard to Find My Way

I decided that it was high time to do what I came here to do. Hell, if folks would have just left me alone, no doubt I would have already figured all this shit out by now. It certainly wasn't *my* fault that I wasn't racing through this case yet.

Since I knew where Morgan had been sitting, and I knew where Liam was, I decided to split the difference. That meant close to the middle where it was the most crowded, which was exactly where I didn't want to be, but I didn't have a whole lot of choice.

I made my way down along the fence that separated the field from the stands. Field side, there sat the team, such as it was. I got my first good look at them, and what I saw was rather underwhelming, I have to say. The few games I had attended over the years usually had, like, five times as many people on the sidelines. Between the coaches, players, cheerleaders, and little kids acting as water boys, there were usually a pile of folks, enough to leave it feeling crowded.

That was not the case here. There was a pretty full roster of cheerleaders, I thought, though I didn't really know how many you're supposed to have. Is there a fixed number? Regardless, I reckoned it was a good policy to not spend much time looking at the underage girls in skirts.

There were only three coaches, though, which I definitely knew wasn't normal. In Jubal County, there are way too many folks clinging onto faded memories of a better time. You could always count on there being a passel of old men who coached so they could get a little taste of those glorious days back when they were young and idolized. For there to only be three grown men on the sidelines? Well, that stood out.

They were all distinct in their own way. The guy who I took to be the head coach, since he was doing the most yelling, was fucking old. Had to be in his late sixties, I guessed, though it didn't seem to be slowing him down any. Looked like he could probably bench-press me—though, strung out as I am, that may not be the biggest accomplishment. Either way, old dude was jacked.

His minions were decidedly not. One guy was maybe five feet tall, and damn near as wide. You don't see suspenders much these days, but he was rocking a pair of hideously bright orange ones. They looked like what Willy Wonka would wear if he became an Auburn fan. He sorta jumped forward to wave his arms around—some sort of signal, no doubt—and I almost flinched in fear that one of the suspenders might pop and take my head clean off on the rebound.

The other coach had red hair.

Ok, so maybe he wasn't that distinctive, but I would like to point out that it was that sort of orangey red, so it kinda looked like it had been dyed to match the school's color. Though, judging by how pale and freckled he was, I suspected it was all natural. But I wasn't about to ask if the curtains matched the drapes.

The few players that weren't on the field were basically just clones of each other. Some a little taller, some a little shorter; some Black, some white; but with their helmets on, it didn't matter. Drones, all of them, just waiting for their chance to go buzzing around the field. Eleven other clone drones were out on the field just then, on defense from the looks of things, so suffice it to say it was only a small cluster of players on the sidelines.

I started to make my way into the stands, and boy, did I catch a couple of glares. Not many, not like I would have at an Elk Grove or even a Sumpville game. But clearly my reputation had preceded me. And being in a mood, I decided to put on a shit-eating grin and sit in one of the few open spots. Which just so happened to be right beside one of the people glaring.

Whoever he was, he was a slightly older man who looked to be in his early forties, sitting with what I guessed was his wife. She didn't pay me no nevermind, but he was clearly incensed; if looks could kill, I'd have been struck dead. He didn't say anything, though. He just cut me one more hard look, then went back to looking at the game. I could tell by the tension in his posture that he hadn't forgot me, though; he was just trying to ignore me.

I thought about saying something. Maybe introducing myself, at least, just to see how he'd react. But I decided I had tempted fate enough, and instead I opted to see if I could detect any magic.

If I had been alone, or just surrounded by my kin, I would have summoned up my little magic sniffing spell and sent it hunting. But that was out. And unless I wanted to walk every inch of this place to see if I could feel any magical energy up close—which I can assure you I did not—then it was going to come down to looking for anything odd.

The crowd looked normal enough, if maybe a little older and more portly than I remembered crowds having been "back in my day." Just a bunch of orange-clad folks, mostly focused on the football before us. There was a steady stream of chatter as folks talked about a little bit of everything all around me. This was a pretty big social event for a town like Burgamy Village, but it all blended together into a mostly steady hum.

I figured what I would be looking for probably wouldn't be in the stands anyway, not unless the folks of this part of the county were a lot more understanding. No, Summerall was pretty sure there was cheating going on, a magical sort, so that would have to be happening out on the field. I just had to spot it.

Reaching into my pocket, I palmed a little bit of mushroom I had packed. I had to work it out of the little sandwich baggie I had placed it in, which in retrospect probably looked like I was fishing around in my pants for something else mushroom shaped. But after a few seconds I had it in hand and, faking a big yawn, popped it in my mouth.

It tasted like dirt, likely from the dirt that was on it, and earth. But I knew in a few minutes it would give me a little hint of just what was going on around me. Just a hint, though, a *little* hint, because I damn sure could not afford to be tripping balls in the middle of a football stadium. I chewed a little, just to mash it into a gritty pulp, then swallowed.

I watched the game vacantly while I waited.

It was ok, I guess. The other team—I still had never figured out who they were—were getting pretty roughly manhandled by the Swampcat defense. I settled in just in time to see the opposing quarterback get sacked so hard, his helmet came off. Pretty sure I saw that kid's soul leave his body for a second, and damned if it didn't look like he wanted to just lay there and die, all to the roar of the crowd around me. It's gotta be something to be a kid and hear a bunch of adults excited because you just almost got knocked the fuck out.

But the kid had far more spunk than I would, 'cause he just staggered to his feet. He even managed to make it into the huddle, with a little help from the guy who I thought was his center. It was kinda hard to read their uniform numbers, though, because their uniforms were stained to hell and back. They'd all been driven into the grass more than their fair share, and it showed.

Soon the kid got back under center, just in time to get sacked again.

Two Swampcats broke through the line damn near as one and smacked that poor QB so hard that I wouldn't have been the least bit surprised if you told me he'd died. Not that any of the Swampcat faithful cared; they were all losing their collective shit, whooping and hollering. I thought they'd been loud after the first sack, but that was just a warm-up. Round two, and even the sourpuss beside me was on his feet shouting to high heaven.

It took him awhile this time, but the no-name quarter-back got to his feet in time to jog off the field so the punt team could come on. I wasn't a coach, but fourth and about thirty isn't something you really come back from. They were just lucky he hadn't been sacked into a safety.

About the time the punt was caught by the Swampcat . . . punt catcher? Hell, I know a little about football, but some stuff just never stuck—but yeah, about the time the punt was caught and run back for about a twenty yard return, the faintest hints of my high were maybe starting to flit around the corners of my vision. Now it was just a waiting game.

I *really* wanted a hot dog. A good one. I was still pissed off about that travesty of a dog I'd paid good money for. Just thinking about how a juicy all-beef frank would feel as I bit into it, a thin line of drizzled mustard dripping onto my tongue . . . damn, I was hungry. I tried thinking back to the last time I ate and realized I couldn't really remember clearly.

Another shout went up from the crowd, but I had missed what it was all about. I was trying to focus—really, I was—but nothing was sticking. I had too much going on in my head: Anna, Morgan, hunger, drugs. It was all just a bit much, and I wanted off the ride. I was crashing hard emotionally, and that was never good. All my anger and annoyance was fading into a dull black depression.

This wasn't working. I'm no fucking detective at the best of times, and this was far from that. I don't know that I'd ever even *had* a "best of times"; my life was basically one never-ending shitstorm of my own creation. I could actually feel some tears starting to come up, and I wasn't about to give the grim fuck beside me the satisfaction.

I got to my feet, barely managing to not trip over my feet as I clambered down the steps of the stands. I had a lot of forward momentum without much direction, as I sort of let gravity do most of the work and kept my head down. I was damn sure not going to let these people see me have a full-blown come-apart. The fact that my hoodie was back at my shed was a ballbuster; I would have loved to have been able to throw the hood up. So instead, I just looked down and kept blinking hard and heavy.

It wasn't till I had made it a good fifty or sixty feet that I realized I was heading the wrong way. When I risked looking up, I came to see that I was out past the press box and concession stand, which was the opposite direction of the car. And to turn around right now would mean walking past anyone who had paid me any attention, and they would probably think I was a damn fool.

Normally I live in a state of not giving a good goddamn what people think. But right then . . . perhaps I was a little fragile.

I decided that I would keep walking, make a lap around the field, and come out by the stadium gate near the car. It was a much longer walk, but there would be a lot fewer people to pass by, the extra time might even give me the chance to clear my head.

That was the plan, at least.

So, of course, it went to shit.

Behind the Stadium with You

I had just about made it to the end of the field when I started paying a little more attention to what was going on around me. Yes, I was leaving, and to hell with this job! But that didn't mean I couldn't solve shit between here and the car. Then I wouldn't have to tell Summerall to fuck off and have to deal with not paying him back what I had already spent.

The drugs felt like they were starting to kick in a bit *morel*, pun intended, for what little amount there was. These were some of the last of my special stash of "See Through the Veil" shrooms, and it would be a shame to let them go to waste, really. Not that there really was an actual veil or anything—at least I didn't think so. I wasn't really sure about all the metaphysics, if I'm being honest. I also wasn't sure when I would be able to get any more of these foul-tasting but surprisingly useful treats . . .

I began to see something moving beneath me, below the surface of the ground. Which naturally was not possible, but then that's magic for you.

I stopped walking for a second and gazed out at the field. Imagine for a moment that you were looking at a spot where an old oak tree had been cut off flat where it rose from the ground. Now imagine you could almost see its roots through the dirt, like you had a real faint negative image of them laid over your vision. That's kinda like what I was seeing.

At the center of the field, around where the two lines of young men were actively squaring off for the next round of bludgeoning, I could see what looked like an underground shadow, not that that makes much sense. In my heightened vision, there were faint translucent red tendrils spread out to cover the whole field. They actually spread out pretty much as far as I could see, to the very edges of light from the stadium, though the farther from the field they got, the thinner and sparser they became.

They went deep, real deep. My depth perception was perhaps a bit off, due to the drugs, but I saw the impression of an inverted tree, almost, and all the while they pulsed ever so faintly. Well, it was less like a pulse and more like the reflection of light on water. Like a silvery shimmer amongst the red.

I heard the Swampcat quarterback yell the count, then "Hike!" The two sides collided into each other with a crunch of shoulder pads, and below the ground the tendrils tensed. I can't explain it any better than to say they looked like they took a deep breath, and then exhaled in time to the quarterback's call. Staring hard, I thought I could see the faintest tinge of red on the feet of the Swampcat players, like they were drawing up whatever those threads were putting out.

Which was probably exactly what they were doing. I mean, not consciously, but there was definitely magic cooking here. Just what it was, however, I had no clue, but it was clear something fucky was afoot. My guess was that whatever spell was at work here was drawing strength from the earth and feeding it into the players. The fact that the tendrils were red was a little troubling, though. That could be a side effect of the drugs, sure, but it could also hint at some sort of blood magic. As the name implies, that's typically not a good thing.

As I watched, I could see that one of the tendrils was darker than the others—much darker. I don't know how something can really glow black, but here it was. It was one tendril that went from the center, back down the length of the field in the direction I had been walking, and then off toward the woods.

I followed that trail with my eyes, over to where I thought I remembered seeing a few people standing earlier. As I watched I thought I could see a little bit of movement, but it wasn't until I saw the red flare of a cigarette being puffed on that I knew for sure that people were still there. I looked from them back to the field.

There was another shout, the start of a play. I saw young men go flying down the field as the Swampcat quarterback dropped back to pass. The no-name defensive line was trying to break through, but it was like they were playing against a wall for as much as they were able to shift the offensive line front four. The QB had all the time in the world, and a pick of targets from the looks of things.

What caught my eye most, though, was that while all those reddish tendrils were mostly staying put—since roots don't move—that one black tendril was shifting. There was a tall, lanky white boy running deep, and with each step that blackness followed along behind him. The team might be getting help from the red, but it was clear this boy had some sort of special relationship with it apart from everyone else.

I wanted to keep walking on out of there, but fuck me if my curiosity wasn't all riled up now. It's one thing when some rich guy tells you to be interested; it's another to actually see the shenanigans right before your eyes. So while I wanted to just keep throwing up my figurative middle finger at this whole affair . . .

Well, curiosity may have killed the cat, but satisfaction brought him back.

My, How You Have Grown

You weren't supposed to smoke on the grounds, but I was far enough away from the masses that I was gonna risk it. Besides, I knew someone up ahead was smoking, too, and I didn't see the SWAT team 'coptering in. I needed to calm my nerves, and while smoking didn't do that exactly, it at least gave my hands something to do. It also wasn't the hardest thing to mask some spell motions by lighting a cig or taking a drag, either.

I weighed calling up a little power, but I wasn't really in the right state of mind to make that call, I figured, so I didn't. I thought that was very responsible of me, to recognize that getting fucked up on hallucinogens in a public forum had perhaps made me a little impaired. Very responsible.

So instead I just dug out a smoke, whisked out my lighter from whatever place the small items I magically whisk away go to, and headed for the woods. I didn't make any move to hide myself. I wanted them to know I was coming, to see if the magic changed any. I wasn't sure what that would tell me exactly, but it might give me some sort of hint.

The light put out by the big stadium lights was muted by the time I got near the tree line. There probably should have been a fence here, 'cause it seemed to me that any ol' sketchy person could just come up out these woods and be on school grounds. But there wasn't, so if that was a testament to poverty or poor judgment, I couldn't tell.

What I could see was that the trees had a gentle sway to them. It was probably the drugs, but they had a sort of pleasing motion to them that made me think of wind chimes. They also seemed to swallow all the light—just gobble it up like it was never there. But I didn't feel scared. I probably ought to have been, but I didn't. I think I was too wrung out emotionally at the moment to feel much else.

Deep in the shadows I could see there were a few forms moving about. I saw another red spark of a cigarette burning, a brief flare of light in an otherwise dark space. I tried listening, but while I thought I might have heard a little murmur before me, it was quickly drowned out by the shouts from the game. That black tendril, though, never wavered.

And then Angie Burdette stomped into view, and I swore.

You would think that saving her life from an insane satyr who thought he was a god would have held me in good stead with the girl. But that's the thing about magic—if you aren't used to it, it has a way of warping your memory sometimes. So while I did in fact save her life, Angie didn't remember it that way. She remembered it more as me stealing her away from her god Cernunos.

I'd long given up trying to explain to her just how badly she didn't want to actually meet Cernunos. If she wouldn't listen to my words nor my scars, then there was nothing I could really do. Ain't no learning some folks.

I knew she and her daddy had moved away—my guess was to get away from the county rumor mill—I had just thought they would have moved farther away than Burgamy fucking Village. At least I hoped they had moved here and that Angie wasn't just visiting. I could not wrap my mind around finally getting away from this hellhole and then coming back to visit.

"You need to go the hell away," Angie hissed at me. She was pissed, and by rights she should have been yelling. But instead she hurled it at me all quiet like, like some sort of rage-filled librarian. The kind of thing you do if you're hiding something.

So I just ignored her, other than to flip her off, and kept walking. I made to walk around her, but she tried to step in front of me, cut me off. I stutter stepped, trying not to run into her. Last thing I needed was to catch a charge for assault.

"Fuck off, Marsh!"

Soon she was in my face, and it suddenly occurred to me that she was bigger than me. Not fat—though basically everyone not strung out on drugs was fatter than me—but she was a little taller, and a lot more solid. Almost like she played sports, which was quite a change from when I had last seen her.

Bigger, angrier, and in my face with it. There was no way around her that I could see, so I had to confront her. Or . . .

I stopped and turned to look back at the field. I could just turn around and walk away, go to the car like I had planned. I mean, sure, I had been paid to take care of this, but near as I could guess, folks probably weren't getting bad hurt. And whatever Angie was caught up in . . . well, that wasn't my business either.

God, I wanted to just leave. But that lingering guilt of how things went with Angie, how maybe if I had handled things differently she might not have wound up getting kidnapped, came bubbling up. She was one hell of a sour bitch, but I felt responsible for her, at least a little. So I bit down the need to flee and turned back.

She was still in my face, still shouting.

I felt responsible, but that damn sure didn't mean I had to like her.

"God, you're a miserable bitch," I muttered. I didn't shout it, but she heard me in spite of her own yelling.

Her eyes widened, nostrils flaring. "Excuse you?"

"You heard me. I know you're up to something, and as usual I bet you are way the fuck out of your depth. Just let me see what's going on, and then I'll go the fuck on. But you know me. You know I ain't leaving until figure shit out."

"Maybe I wouldn't have to be such a bitch to you if you weren't such a fucking jackoff! Don't you have some meth to be cooking?"

Over her shoulder I saw another figure come out of the gloom. This was someone I didn't know, and judging from their clothes, I probably didn't want to. They looked like someone had puked up the fall lineup from Hot Topic on them, then mixed in a few dog leashes for good measure. Whoever they were, as they got closer I was fairly sure it was a man. This guy was a lot taller than me but rail thin. Honestly, we might have weighed about the same, even though he was at least six inches taller. And to top it all off, his hair was dyed the same dumb orange color as the Swampcats, only spiked up into a shitty Mohawk.

"Hey, calm down Moonfire," he said. One hand was wrapped across his chest while the other sort of tugged at the dog collar around his neck.

I couldn't help but laugh. "Moonfire? Of fucking course. God, you are just the fucking worst, you know that?"

She slapped me.

Sometimes I'm Overcome Thinking 'Bout It

To my credit, I just took it, even if it was mostly because I didn't have a lot of choice. She rocked me back on my heels, fucking staggered me. I felt my jaw pop, and I was lucky she didn't dislocate it. If I'd known she was that strong, I might have been a little less lippy.

Then again, knowing me, I'd have ran my mouth anyway.

She didn't come in for seconds, so I just stood there out of arm's reach, rubbing my jaw. I tasted a little blood, but running my tongue across the inside of my mouth I could tell I'd kept all of my few remaining teeth. "Aight then," I spat.

"I'm not playing with you. Go away." She sounded a little calmer now, and I could see in her eyes that she was really uncomfortable with what she'd just done. Which was good—maybe that meant she wouldn't do it again. At least I hoped so.

I held up both hands, trying to look peaceful. I decided to reign things in a bit, see if I couldn't reason with her. "I can't. Y'all are doing something magic, and I have to at least see what. Make sure y'all are being safe, at least."

Carrot Top somehow managed to look even more skittish. "Who is he?" he hissed at Angie, trying to be quiet, but not so hard that I couldn't hear him.

"I'm a guy who knows things," I said the same time as Angie said, "He's an asshole."

"Both," I added after. "I mean, she's not wrong. I'm a righteous prick, loser, addict, yadda yadda. But I know a lot more about whatever shit y'all are doing back in those woods than anyone else you're gonna come into contact with."

I thought about Morgan then and knew that wasn't true. I began to wonder if whatever was going on here was why she had shown up, if even now she was cutting through the dark like some sort of magic shark, coming to gobble these kids up. I thought of Kandra, the girl she killed, and a chill ran down my spine. I glanced around anxiously, but all the movement I could see was probably drug fueled.

"No. You've already ruined my one good thing, I'm not gonna let you ruin this too." Angie crossed her arms, suddenly looking a lot older than her eighteen years. Stern. Very "angry punk mom" vibe.

I huffed. "Look, I promise not to interfere if y'all are being safe. But there are things you don't know, things that might come along that are a lot less nice than me. The kinds of things that don't stop and talk, just go to ripping out throats."

A female voice came from out of the darkness, from behind where Angie and Tall Boy had come from. "Let him past, Ang."

Tall Boy, who was looking around now, nodded. "Just let him look, ok? It's not like it's bad. All this is gonna draw attention. If someone tells my mom I was hanging out in the woods instead of watching the game . . ."

"God, you're such a loser, Lucas."

"Lucasfer!" he corrected instantly.

"I take it back. *He's* the fucking worst." I couldn't even muster a laugh at that. It was too awful. I prayed right then and there that I hadn't been that much of a travesty when I was his age.

Angie just rolled her eyes and turned away from me. She brushed past Lucas(fer) and faded into the darkness. My eyes were a little better adjusted now, but then I was still high, so that didn't mean as much as it probably should have. I could at least see vague shapes amongst the trees now.

Lucas realized that he was the only thing separating me from where I wanted to be and, I swear to God, he squeaked. It was pitiful. And awkward. I was glad when he followed behind Angie, and I wished he would just keep on going so I wouldn't have to deal with whatever it was he had going on.

I stepped into the tree line and let the darkness of the thick pines envelop me. The thing about woods is, left to their own devices, they tend to be somewhat open, airish. Throw some humans in the mix, complete with lawnmowers and a complete aversion to limbs of any sort, and what you end up with is a much thicker bit of woods filled with all manner of sticks and brush. But only for a little bit. After that first few feet it becomes less thick once more, and that's what I was walking through.

Some people had worn a little trail into the earth, and that was what I followed, but to either side of me I could see several years' worth of tree trash. It gave me the impression of walking past a row of teeth, headed right down the gullet of something nasty. It was not a good feeling, to say the least.

By about ten feet in, the worst of it was past and the woods seemed a little less grim. They were still dark, but the light that shone through the trees felt more natural.

I caught the odd glimpse of the half-full moon overhead before I reached where I was going. I started to smell a combination of weed and cigarettes, which felt a little like home.

It wasn't a clearing; it was just a space between a few old pines. One of the trees looked like it had been lighting struck, which had left it charred and broken off about fifteen feet up. The rotting remains of the tree had mostly clumped around its base, though a few thick chunks had been arranged in a loose circle, no doubt as seats. The ground was littered with what looked like hundreds of cigarette butts of varying ages. Clearly this had been a smoke spot for years.

There were three people besides me in the space—Angie, Lucas, and another girl who looked a little younger. I guessed they were all around seventeen, eighteen maybe, and each of them dressed in some form of mall goth attire. It was actually kinda adorable, in a totally ridiculous way.

At least it would have been, were it not for the pentagram that had been painted on the forest floor in blood.

Smells Like Teen Spirit

I pointed to the pentagram. "The hell is that?"

"Lucasfer" looked over at Angie. "I thought this guy knew stuff?" he whispered.

"It's a pentagram," said the other girl.

I wanted to bury my face in my hands. "No shit, Sherlock, I know what a pentagram is! What I'm asking is why the hell you used blood to make it? And where did you get the blood?"

Angie shook her head. "It's not blood, it's paint." She walked over to one of the whole trees and produced a small bucket of red paint, complete with a brush sticking out of it. I had to think that paint was good and ruined—hell, it was probably half full of pine needles after using the brush to paint on the ground—but I guess it was better than them using blood. I'd been worried I'd stumbled right into a bunch of psychopaths.

Stepping closer, I bent over and put a finger in it, then smelled my fingertip. *Yep, that's paint.* Now that I looked at it, it was too bright to be blood, even if it was in that half-dry sticky phase. I wiped the paint off as best I could on the little bit of grass nearby and did a piss-poor job.

"Hey, don't touch that!" the other girl protested while I did all that. I obviously ignored her, but she continued, talking to Angie now. "He shouldn't touch that. What if he breaks the seal or whatever?"

Wherever Angie went, she managed to get some flunkies. She might be a magical idiot, and about as pleasant as a mud-covered skunk, but she had something to her, at least. Drive, maybe? I could respect that, I reckoned.

I still thought she was just fucking awful, though.

"You didn't summon something up, right?" I asked. I knew they didn't, of course; if they had somehow managed to actually summon a real live demon or the like, they would already be dead. That pentagram they'd drawn wouldn't hold an imp with a limp. And salt worked a lot better for that anyway, though I didn't have the damnedest clue why.

"I'm not telling you what we did. You're the expert—take a look and see we aren't hurting anyone, and then go the hell on," Angie said.

I flipped her a bird, which . . . hell, it felt small even for me. "Fine. Let me see, then."

I took to looking harder at the scene, really honing in, and tried feeding a little of my power into the drugs fucking me up. It didn't really work, but I could see myself start to glow just a little as I tapped into my power, real faint. I knew none of them would be able to see it, so I wasn't worried. They'd have to be casting a spell or taking some of the same drugs as me to catch a glimpse.

It was dark here, but I could still see that tendril of darkness heading off toward the field. It was flowing down from the center of that pentagram, and I swear I caught the scent of electricity in the air for a second. And under that . . . char. From the side of the pentagram above ground, I could see two very small tendrils flowing. One came from that dead tree, which must have still been tied to the earth just a bit, and the other . . . well, it was coming right out the center of Angie. Right about where her heart was.

The more I learned about magic, the more I realized that specifics, a lot of the time, don't matter as much as the intent and symbols used in support of that intent. That's what made spell jars work, for example—that and a little bit of power. And I think these idiots had stumbled into a perfect vortex that actually made their spell work when, by all rights, it shouldn't have.

So Angie had a tiny touch of power, it seemed. That actually cleared up why she had been able to just stumble into the King like she did, why she had felt drawn to something she probably couldn't ever put into words. But that little seed of power wasn't enough to do something like *this*.

She had gotten lucky, and she was piggybacking off whatever that big spell out on the field was. Not that she knew it. Had that not been going on, her magic would have just shot its wad to no end. And that tree, it just happened to be close enough and in some way tied to what these idiots were trying to accomplish. Making someone "fast as lightning," maybe? I had to wonder if they were that clever; I hadn't been. Hell, I probably still wasn't.

"My guess? You cast a spell on someone. One of the players out there, one of the Swampcats. Something to juice him up, make him faster. That about right? One of y'all's boyfriends?"

Lucasfer's jaw dropped. "Woah."

The two girls looked at each other, Angie very much with a "keep your mouth shut" look on her face, while the nameless girl looked a little scared. She was mouthing something at Angie, but I couldn't tell what it was between the drugs and the dark.

"Damn, I'm good," I said, my mood picking up for the first time all night. I pulled out a cigarette and lit it, basking in a nicotine glow as the Three Stooges had a mini freak-out.

The Goth Kid Who Won Most School Spirit

"**M**an, how did you do that?" Lucas marveled, oblivious to the daggers Angie was shooting in his direction.

I just shrugged. I wasn't about to explain myself, especially not to him. "So what's my prize?"

"Your prize is getting to leave here without us kicking your ass," Angie spat. "So go."

I raised my hands. "Look, I don't actually care what you're doing, so long as you aren't breaking any laws to do it."

"Pretty sure that magic isn't covered by the cops," the younger girl sneered, her voice dripping with sarcasm. "So we're good, then."

"Those aren't the kind of laws I'm talking about." In truth, there were probably all sorts of laws concerning magic; it was just that no one had ever really bothered to teach them to me. What I did know were Granny's laws, and those weren't to be fucked with. One of them was no blood magic—unless she was the one doing it. And if you did do blood magic, you could expect to hear from her in person sooner or later. If you were smart, you went to her and gave her something expensive as penance. If she had to come to you, well, things like as much wouldn't go so smooth.

"A higher law," Lucas said reverentially. He was like some drugged-up cultist the way he was looking at me.

"What? No! I just need to know what you used to cast the spell, and to let you asshats know that if you keep doing magic, sooner or later my granny is gonna have words with you."

Angie scoffed. "Your granny? Right. She as methed out as you?"

I blanched as she said it. I had a visual of what it might look like if someone said something like that to the old crone's face, and it wasn't pretty. Only Krista could get away with that, and even then, not often. "I'd be real careful talking about her. She has a way of hearing things you wouldn't think possible. Ask around enough, and you'll catch wind of what I mean."

The kids looked unnerved. Angie, the least of them, but there was at least something approaching a thoughtful look on her face. She gave a little nod, then motioned to the paint on the ground. "Well, all we used were words and this pentagram. That's it."

That wouldn't have normally worked, I didn't think, but again, these were special piggybacking circumstances. "You got them written down?"

Lucas pulled out a piece of printer paper that had been folded up into a smaller square. Taking a step toward me, he thrust it into my hands. "You can have my copy," he said, way too eager.

I opened it up and gave it a quick glance. Looked mostly like bullshit to me, but whatever. I'd give it a closer look later. "Tumblr?" I said, looking over at Angie.

"I told you, they know what they're talking about there."

I rolled my eyes. "Sure." Hell, maybe they did. Not like I had ever been on there.

I started to turn and leave. I mean, really none of this concerned me, and it's not like I was the magic police. If I was going to do anything, it would be stopping the big magic out on the field, not this piddly shit. Taking that out would end this, anyway. Two birds with one stone and all that.

Angie, though . . . she might prove to be an issue in the future.
It wasn't likely that she would end up being some briar
witch. I really doubted she had enough magic to go down
that path, or else I would have picked up on it. But, again
. . . not really my problem. At least not yet. If she worked
up some small mischief, that was a problem for Granny.

I digested that for a moment. I didn't like her, but I didn't
want her to wind up on Granny's or Morgan's bad side.
Kandra still lingered on my mind, and no one deserved
that fate. So, I looked over at the young woman and tried
to look as disarming as possible. I didn't smile—that
wouldn't get me on anyone's good side—but I did try to
work a little kindness into my eyes. "Aight, then, y'all
have at it. Don't let me stop you. Angie, can we talk for
a second?"

I took a step back toward the edge of the woods and
made a sort of waving gesture toward them. Angie just
crossed her arms. With every ounce of willpower I had, I
resisted the urge to curse and instead managed to squeeze
a muted "please" from between my few remaining teeth.
And wonder of wonders, she huffed, but she followed.

I didn't say anything at first, instead just walking forward
and occasionally glancing back to make sure that Angie,
and just Angie, was following. Still, I waited until we were
out of the woods before I turned to face her once again.

"Fuck do you want?" she demanded, keeping her voice low. She glanced out toward the field, but I didn't see anyone heading our way. Everyone was still focused on the game, and as for me, I could still see those tendrils flowing up into the players. Creepy, but not unexpected at this point.

"I just wanted to warn you. You keep playing around with stuff like this, and it's probably going to go bad for you."

"I think I've done fine so far," she said. "I spent time with my God, no thanks to you."

I wasn't about to beat that dead horse. "You know that girl that got killed not too long ago? That animal attack?"

Angie nodded. "Yeah, I heard about that."

"Yeah, it wasn't an animal. And the woman who killed her is here tonight. You keep fucking around with this stuff, you're going to get caught up in something else you aren't prepared for. And next time, like as not, I won't be around to bail you out, because that woman is a lot more powerful than me."

She took to looking around at that, but seeing as there wasn't some big panther stalking up on us, least that I could see, I reckoned she was safe for the moment. "You're so full of it."

I shrugged, taking one last drag on my cigarette before flicking it into the grass. "Usually, yeah. Not now, though, not that you'll believe me. I'm just gonna hope you're smart enough to think it through."

"That it? All you needed to say?"

God, she was a prickly one. Was this what it was like trying to talk sense into me? Was she some sort of karmic justice inflicted upon me for decades of orneriness? Had to say, I wasn't a fan. "Last question, just cause I'm curious, then I'll leave you losers to it. Why the fuck are a bunch of goth kids even at a football game, much less working magic to help out someone playing in it?"

She got a real fire in her eyes then, and I instantly knew I wasn't about to get any information worth a damn. "What, freaks like me can't have school spirit?"

"Fuck me, forget I asked," I relented, striding away. I wasn't that curious, not enough to deal with Captain Crotchety. It was a boyfriend or crush they were trying to help, I decided. Had to be. So, mystery solved.

I didn't glance back, because I damn sure didn't want her thinking I cared, but around the time I made it to the edge of the football field I did venture a little look. She must have stepped back into the trees, because she was gone from view.

Lord, What Am I Doing Here?

I had thought my mood was getting better, but really it was about the same now that I didn't have those idiot kids to distract me. I decided, though, that even if I was feeling like shit, there wasn't any real reason not to try and nip this whole thing in the bud. Liam had brought me here, and I didn't have a clue when I might be able to get another ride back out this way, what with Anna—

Immediately, I tried to think about anything else. I didn't want to reflect on what life without her might look like, mostly because I already knew exactly what it looked like: day after day of unending bullshit and boredom. To go back to that after a few months of things actually looking up? No, sir. I didn't think I had it in me.

So I took to watching the game instead. I leaned up against one of the aged wooden posts that held up the scoreboard and sorta blended into the shadows, in hopes that it might work and folks like Morgan might not pay me no nevermind. It was weird watching a game from that angle after a lifetime of watching games from the sides. It made it seem a little more personal in a weird way.

While the drugs were still working, I was able to pick out which of the players the Three Amigos had worked their magic on. He was a tallish white kid who was playing receiver while on offense and Ironmanning it to play linebacker on defense. That magic was clearly doing him some good, as his lungs didn't seem to be blown slam out from playing almost nonstop. And he was pretty damn fast. He had this long black hair that flowed out from under his helmet and whipped in the wind when he got to moving.

Fuck if he didn't make me feel tired just watching him.

I kept glancing over to the home side stands, keeping an eye on Morgan as best I could. I was far enough away that she sort of just blended into the crowd, for the most part. I did watch as, right before halftime, she got up and went to the concession stand. No doubt she was trying to beat the rush, but having had one of those travesty dogs they were slinging, I couldn't imagine there being too much of a rush.

I'd seen some weird shit over the past half hour or so, but watching her actually scarf down one of those abominations was the worst by far. She ate it while staring right at me from near where we'd had our little chat earlier. Just locked onto me, not once looking away, as she ate every inch of that dog in what had to be some sort of intense power move.

I guess when you've taken an actual bite out of a human, like she did with Kandra, what was eating a casing filled with peckers and lips?

She ate it down to the last bite, then threw the trash away, never breaking eye contact the whole time. Then she went back to where she was sitting and I pretty well lost her again. Thankfully?

Then it was halftime, and I had things to do.

HALFTIME, AND THE LIVING'S EASY

By "things to do," that mostly meant shifting slightly to the side, because behind me and to my left was the field house where the players did whatever it was they did while they were getting ready. When halftime hit, every player and coach started streaming in my direction so they could go yell at each other or something. Maybe eat a peach. Hell if I knew.

I was pretty sure eating peaches kept you from getting cramps. Not that I'd ever done that, because I pretty well lived my life avoiding any situation where I might stumble into a cramp. Cramps usually meant you'd been running, or lifting, and damned if either of those were my speed.

But peaches aside, they were all heading in my direction, and as I was pretty sure that I was close to being in the way. I mean, I wasn't exactly in their path, leaned up against the pole like I was, but I could see they would be trotting on past pretty close. And to be honest, I was pretty sure this night might end with me needing to avoid as much notice as possible. I decided to shift more in the direction of the Three Losers in the woods in an effort to keep off people's radars.

I did get a better look at the extra special player, but other than getting to see his sweat a little more up close, there wasn't really anything to make note of. Oh, that and he had those little black smears under his eyes like the pro players wore, and they had some sort of writing on them real small. Looked like some numbers, but I wasn't about to walk up and ask him.

But I wasn't lingering here to look at the players; I was here to look at the coaches! Because the way I figured, one of them had to be behind things. I wasn't sure how—that would come to me later, I hoped—but there was no way that one of these kids was working this sort of magic. And who else would be so motivated to win a fucking football game that they would go to the trouble to do this? It had to be a coach pulling the strings, hiring someone to whip this spell up.

I just hoped it wasn't Morgan doing it. Because I damn sure wasn't gonna stop her if she was.

My sight beyond sight didn't reveal anything magically special about any of the three coaches. The short tubby one had long given up on running with the rest of the team, so he was bringing up the rear. The redhead was around the middle of the pack, just sort of lopping along on those long legs of his, and then toward the front was Old Man Head Coach who, despite his age, was pounding along like a Mack truck. He looked like he would have ran slap over me and not even blinked had I been in the way.

And then they were inside the field house, and I had nothing to watch anymore. Now I was just a weirdo standing alone near the end zone, twiddling my thumbs and wishing I was drunk. I could see those spreading tendrils of power still pulsing up from the middle of the vast green of the field, though they were beginning to fade a bit as my shroom-enhanced vision began to wear off. I knew that whatever was causing this would mean I had to check that spot out—something no one was going to let me do willy-nilly with a stadium full of folks.

Wanting a beer plus not being able to do what I needed, multiplied by being a fucking sad sack, equaled going back to the car to work up a drunken state until the game was over, I decided. It wasn't a great plan, I admit, but I think by this point it's pretty clear I haven't ever had one of those, so why start now?

WE'D FINALLY BE GETTING DOWN TO IT, BUT I'M AN ORNERY SHIT

It's safe to say I got quite some fucking looks cut at me. Sitting on the trunk with a beer in your hand, a few crushed empties on the ground at your feet, will do that, I reckon. I don't know why everyone was so upset, though. It was like everyone thought their precious kids had never seen a drink before, as though half those parents weren't going to crack one open as soon as they got home, if not in the car on the way there. *Pretentious bastards.*

I had been pacing myself best I could, and I'd only had seven or so, to my recollection. Likely a bit more than my fair share of the beer Liam and I had brought, but what can you do? Damn things leapt right into my hand. What was I supposed to do, insult them by putting them back in the case? Not me; I couldn't bear to hurt their feelings like that.

Anyway, I was feeling good. And holding it together well enough. I'd had a little cry in the car when no one was around, but after the end of the third quarter folks started to trickle out of the stadium, so I dried my eyes and got out. Figured a bit of fresh air and all that would help the drinking, and it did. I tried calling Anna again, but she didn't answer. She did respond to a text of mine, at least, saying we'd talk tomorrow—which could go either way, I reckoned.

If I had been a bit less drunk, I would've probably sat there and worried myself into a complete come-apart. But I was dancing that finest of lines between being drunk and not worrying and being so drunk that I got all in my feels. Call me a sumbitchin' mental ballerina.

It pays to be good at something.

As the game wrapped up—with the score fifty-three to three, some overly excited soul told me in passing—the trickle soon became a stream of folks heading to their cars. Which only increased the number of hard looks I got. The real highlight was when some guy I didn't recognize sent his friends on walking but hung back to tell me just what a disgrace I was.

"If we weren't in public, I'd whup your ass, Marsh" was about the nicest thing he said to me. And if you think he was receptive to the bird I flipped him as I downed the last of my beer, well, you'd be mistaken. He had his Salt Life hat flipped backwards in about two seconds flat, then whipped his T-shirt off without losing the hat, revealing a too-tight wifebeater. Clearly the public nature of our discourse wasn't the detriment to fighting that it had been just moments before. Call it magic.

Now that's when Liam showed up and got between us. He put a hand on the old boy's chest and started talking calm-like, trying to defuse things. It might have even worked, but unfortunately for all parties concerned, I had just finished my beer. And that's when the devil on my shoulder won out in a big way.

I tossed the empty and, I swear to whatever god you want me to, it smacked Salt Life right square in the forehead.

It was a thing of absolute beauty. That silver can flung through the air, a few drops of spilling beer catching the light of a nearby car's headlights, flicked right over Liam's shoulder, and landed with a thump about two inches below the turned-back cap.

For a moment, everything froze. Old Boy's eyes went about as wide as the bottom of the can that had just hit him. Liam looked back at me, a look that spoke endless volumes of "What the hell?" And me? I just took the hand that had just tossed the can, made a fist, and then popped up my middle finger.

Then all hell broke loose.

And Then All Hell Broke Loose

R edneck rage is a very real thing.

Salt Life turned into the Incredible Hulk about a heartbeat later. Liam didn't stand a chance, and he was just lucky that I was the target. Old Boy, with one hand, shoved Liam to the side so hard that my friend collapsed to the ground. It was fast, too—one second there was someone between me and the asshole, and then there wasn't anything but air and opportunity.

Then Salt Life let loose a roar that stole all the air.

Two quick steps later he was on me. I had started trying to get down off the trunk, but he beat me to it. Then he beat me off it. I felt a fist hit my jaw so hard, it popped. If I'd had teeth there, I think they would have fallen out. As it was, the rest of me did fall out; I was smacked right off the trunk with the force of the blow, knocking me onto the ground below. To add insult to injury, the case of beer must have gotten tipped over, because a second later full cans of beer began to rain down on me as they rolled off the top of the car.

I tried to push myself to my feet, but before I could even get my arms under me, a boot hit my gut. It hurt like hell and took all the air from me, leaving me trying to gasp for air. I could feel that I was going to be sick, all that beer in my belly having just been good and riled up. Ever need to throw up but not have any breath? It's hell. But that was the least of my problems.

What little sense I had told me to try and get away, so I tried to roll under the car. It almost worked, but I was farther up toward the road than I thought and my shoulder hit the back tire, stopping me from getting good and hid. Not that he was going to give me a chance—I felt hands grabbing at my ankles, and I started trying to thrash so he couldn't get a firm grip.

I felt my foot connect with something, maybe a hand, and heard Salt Life swear. The pain clearly didn't hold him back, though, as a moment later he clamped on tight to both of my ankles, one hand on each, and took to pulling. The only lucky thing I had going for me was that the ground here was grass, not gravel. It still didn't feel great, but that was such a minor pain in that moment that it hardly registered.

I tried grabbing onto the tire but couldn't get a grip. I tried to twist my body so I would be on my back, at least, but my shoulder hit the underside of the car, knocking me back flat. And then I was out from under the car, the yellow glow of the nearest streetlight hitting me. I started to curl in on myself as best I could, hands and arms protectively pulled over my head and face.

The hands turned loose from my ankles, and I heard a grunt. Looking up from between my arms, I could see that Liam had gotten to his feet and shoved my attacker off of me. The redneck hadn't fallen over, but he had been staggered back far enough that there was some space between us all now.

I started to get to my feet and scuttle behind the car at the same time. A little cover was high on my wish list just then so I could either take a moment to puke my guts out or plan an escape route. Liam and the redneck were shouting back and forth, but I wasn't paying much attention to the words flying as I battled my own guts. I could tell that Liam was trying to calm things down, at least as best you can calm anything down by shouting.

Salt Life shifted his focus back to me. Telling Liam to get fucked, he whipped his wifebeater off over his head, flinging it and the hat caught up in it behind him. It revealed a disturbing number of ab muscles, I noticed, right before he started to lunge in my direction. I'm not ashamed to admit I flinched. Old Boy clearly wasn't a stranger to weight lifting, judging from the pounding in my jaw, and I didn't fancy being his punching bag.

That said, I ain't totally afraid of a fight, so rather than turn and run I squared up. I was gonna go down swinging this time, even if it cost me the rest of my teeth. But Liam, actual fucking good dude that he was, went to get between us again, his hand up and palms out. Still trying to stop this before shit got even more sideways than it already was.

That was when Salt Life dropped an N-bomb.

And then Liam proceeded to whip that dude's ass like he'd stolen something.

Mistakes Were Made

I could feel Liam glaring a hole in the side of my head.

The way things played out, I reckoned I was lucky we were all handcuffed, and not together. There was still a chance he could headbutt me, or bite me maybe, but for now he just seemed content to glare at me.

"Sometimes I really hate you," he said in a low voice.

"Shhh!" I hissed. I was trying to listen to the cops, who were standing about twenty feet away, discussing our fate. Until they put us in the back of the cop car, we stood a chance, and I needed to know if there was enough wiggle room for me to work a little magic.

Salt Life wasn't making it easy, though. He was leaned up against the other cop car, also handcuffed, which explained why he wasn't wiping the blood from his pretty clearly broken nose. Liam had given him an abject lesson on exactly why racism is real fucking dumb. However, that didn't stop Old Boy from dropping a few more slurs from where he was standing, but they lost a lot of their sting when said through a mouthful of blood.

Goddamn, though, rednecks can cuss. He was saying things that I was pretty sure were reeeeal racist, but I didn't have the beginning of a context to be able to figure out what the hell he meant. I was sorta thankful that Liam seemed to be more focused on me, as much as it can be a good thing when one of your only friends is real pissed at you. But it at least meant he wasn't making the situation worse by trying to fight Salt Life in handcuffs.

"I know you did not just shush me," he said, clearly getting angrier.

I leaned my head close and whispered as low as I could, where I thought he could still hear, "Look, I'm trying to get us out of this. Beat my ass later, once the cops have let us loose."

He looked like he wanted to say some more, but I could feel his body tense as he managed to choke the words back. He looked up, and I was pretty sure he was praying then, his lips moving soundlessly. Probably praying for patience, since he was in this shit entirely because of me.

I felt real bad about that—I really, really did. But I couldn't focus on that right then. I could ask forgiveness later. Right now, I needed to make things right if I could.

Someone like Granny, or probably Morgan, they can change memory and compel people if they need to. It's not easy, but it is possible. Me, I can only nudge folks a little, and only if they were sorta already leaning that way to begin with. If these cops were, say, not really feeling like dealing with the paperwork, then maybe I could work that. But I needed to hear how they were feeling. I also really needed them to not search Liam's car too in depth, because that would be all she wrote. Luckily, I was pretty sure that Burgamy Village PD was too poor to have a drug dog. So as long as they didn't call in the sheriff's department, and I knew all too well they had one, we would be fine there.

One cop was a short Black man who had an ex-military look about him; the other, an older white guy, had a real seventies-looking pedo 'stache. It looked like they were wrapping up the debate, and I thought I had heard a lot of tiredness in their tone. Maybe the games were overtime? It's not like there could be all that big of a force down here.

They split then, each of them going toward their own cruiser, which meant we were blessedly stuck with Pedo 'Stache. I figured a military guy was probably more of a stickler for the rules, and someone blessed with this absolute unit of a lip sweater couldn't be that much of a hardass. As if he could sense my eyes drifting jealously across his whiskers, he reached up and ran his thumb and forefinger across it. Picture someone deep in thought, really weighing the options, with a mustache crafted by the gods to keep an upper lip perfectly warm for all eternity. It was *exactly* like that.

He hitched his belt up a bit as he rolled up on us, and for the first time I had a second to read his badge. Mitchell, it read, which didn't really ring any bells. But then I wasn't from here, so why would it?

"Well, guys . . ." Mitchell started.

Leaned back against the car like I was, my hands were hidden from view. The moment he had started heading our way, I had taken to working my fingers in the patterns I had learned as a child, damn near my first and most useful spell. One learned at the feet of my grandpa, his worn hands wrapped around my own to help me shape the complex forms this spell required. I poured a steady trickle of my magic into it as I did, building it up in power. This was a small working, so there was only so much I could feed into it. It would either work or it wouldn't, and the amount of power I used had little to do with that.

"You gonna turn us loose, Chief?" I asked, letting that spell flow out across my tongue and into his ears, where hopefully it would root in his brain.

He started to shake his head a little. "Well, even if I wanted to, you know how it is. Kids' football game and all that." His voice was as tired as I'd thought it was from afar. And he wasn't saying a direct no . . . maybe there was still a chance.

I kept my fingers working, still trickling in that power. It's hard to explain, but sometimes magic is as much about feel as anything. A spell like this was less about bludgeoning them into submission as it was about slipping in a suggestion, just weaseling it inside the ol' brainbox. "You heard what they said, right?" I asked, twiddling away.

"They" were a pair of older women who had happened to be walking by right when Salt Life lost his shit. Luckily they had missed me tossing the beer can, because sometimes God does favor fools. Seeing as they were the only two to hang around and give a statement, I thought we came off looking pretty good.

"Yeah, we did. And I'm sympathetic," he said, nodding toward Liam. "I am. But no matter what someone says, you can't just go to wailing on them right beside a school. We're not . . ."

The whole time he'd been speaking, Mitchell had been having to get louder and louder as Salt Life proceeded to absolutely lose his goddamn mind. Clearly he wasn't taking the fact that he was getting arrested well, and while I commiserated, I really needed him to calm the fuck down so that he didn't get these cops riled past the point where my magic might work.

". . . able to just let folks . . ."

That's when the shouting stopped long enough for the sound of that redneck bastard hocking a wad of blood in the other cop's face to reach my ears. The three of us all looked over just in time to see Salt Life launch a headbutt that struck right into the chin of Mitchell's partner, knocking him on his ass. He punctuated it with another string of slurs as he turned to run off into the darkness. He was whooping up a storm, and not for the first time I began to suspect that he might have been under the influence. It was goddamn amateur hour up in Burgamy Village.

Long hair streaming out from beneath his hat, Salt Life sprung for freedom, the sweat glistening across his broad shoulders. Like some sort of two-legged whitetail, he dove for the freedom of the far side of the road, high-stepping so fast that his work boots were a blur of motion. He wasn't what you'd call conventionally handsome, but in that moment, he was a thing of beauty.

Mitchell was older, but fuck, he was quick. And for once in my life I got to see a Taser in action—and not on my own flesh. Mitchell had it drawn in a split fucking second, and before Salt Life could get more than fifteen, twenty feet away, those wires shot out. They hit high in the runner's back, right between his shoulder blades, which were all scrunched up together thanks to his hands being cuffed behind him.

He dropped like a stone. Well, a stone having a seizure, maybe. Salt Life hit the pavement with a thud and took to flopping as Mitchell leaned into that trigger. He was not fucking around, and it took everything in me to not egg him on.

Ex-Military had gotten to his feet and as soon as Mitchell had laid off the sparks, he dove onto Salt Life, planting a knee in his back to pin him down. Not that the redneck was going anywhere; he'd been taken slap out the game. That didn't stop the cop on his back from giving him a discrete few smacks, though—you know, just to make sure he stayed down and stopped resisting.

"Fuck," Liam murmured, so low only I could hear him.

Agreed.

Mitchell started calling things in over his radio, which caught my attention hard and heavy. I'd learned before that until they called it in, nothing was real. You weren't arrested, you hadn't been pulled over, none of that—not really. As long as our names didn't cross that man's lips as he called this event in to dispatch, then I'd know we were going home tonight.

I worked my fingers like never before. As far as I knew, you had to actually speak words for this to work. But I was stuck: I didn't want him to think about us at all, not even glance in our direction, yet I wanted this spell to work.

So, I just worked the magic and . . . thought it at him. Real hard.

And when he clicked off from the radio, he'd only called in the tussle with Salt Life.

We were going free.

Nope

"Nope," Liam said, rolling up the window the last crack.

I was standing outside the passenger side door. Which was locked. Intentionally, I had just found out.

A million words ran across my brain, but none of them reached my tongue. Without another word, I watched as Liam put the car in drive. I just stood there silently as he pulled a three-point turn, then drove off into the night, leaving me alone.

The nearby parking lot was mostly empty, save for a couple of older model trucks and one shitty little Caprice. The side of the road where the rest of the cars had parked was just as empty, with only a beat-up S10 to keep me company. I was pretty sure there was someone in it, but I wasn't paying it any attention, really. I was more concerned with the fact my cell phone was dead as hell.

I was in my feels in a big way. I wasn't crying yet, but I was pretty sure the tears were coming. Tonight had been nothing but one unending string of fuck-ups, and even though I was frantically trying to figure out ways they weren't my fault . . . they were. I only had about five people in my life that cared about me: my uncle, my cousin, my drug dealer, my girlfriend, and Liam. And from the way things looked, I was now down two of them. And can you really even count your drug dealer? Would Jimmy actually have hung out with me if not for the money he leeched from me?

The fact that I hadn't even had a chance to get my stuff out of the car dawned on me suddenly, and I swore.

I knew that HD was probably on his way, or at least he would be. His own little power would be telling him that I was needing him, and he'd come on soon enough. But it would be a bit, so I had a choice: I could hold a big ol' pity party there on the side of the road . . .

. . . or I could sneak back in the stadium, do what Summerall wanted, and at least make the night profitable in some way.

It took a minute of internal wrangling, but in the end I decided that if I got cracking on pretty quickly, I'd have time to do both before HD showed. So with a sigh, I started for the gate.

Breakers Roar

The gate, such as it was, wasn't really designed to keep people out. It had been built with vehicles in mind, so in the end all I actually had to do was just sort of duck low and weasel under it. Certainly not my first break-in, but by far my easiest, I had to admit. If they were all that quick and painless, I reckoned I would be a lot richer.

Probably have a few less arrests, too, for that matter.

I didn't see anyone around, but that didn't have me too surprised. Getting sorted with the cops took a good bit longer than I would have thought, considering they were turning us loose. Mitchell had decided that a fuck-off long lecture was our penance, I guessed, because I thought I was going to die of boredom by the time he finished.

Then Liam and I had our thing. Lots of shouting, a good bit of pleading, some surprisingly sincere apologizing that went unbelieved. That old chestnut. So I guessed by now it was easily more than an hour after the game was over, and things were pretty well shut down from the looks of it.

The stadium was totally empty. The only movement to be seen was what looked like some sort of paper tumbling across the ground, caught by the wind. It was pretty dark, too, what with all the lights turned off, even the scoreboard. In fact, the only light I could see was the faintest crack coming from the field house door. It was pretty far off, but I thought it looked like it was propped open. Maybe a coach was still puttering around in there.

That was a bit of a wrinkle, seeing as there was no place to hide once I was on the field proper. And I was certain that was where I needed to be to get at this thing, whatever it was, so I could either wait, or just risk it.

I decided to risk it. The way my luck was running, I figured it was just as likely the earth would just open up and swallow me whole, which would be nice. Get me free of all the bullshit in my head for good. As an added bonus, no one would ever really know what happened to me, and that would serve them right.

It was a shitty, petty thought, but that's where my mind was. I actually started to get really mad. I knew I should have been mad at myself, but fuck that; I decided that I was going to be mad at whatever was lurking out there under the field. Whatever was going on, that was what set all these things in motion, these things that had gone so shittily for me.

I struck a trot for the center of the field. With none of the proper drugs flowing in me, I could no more see those tendrils than you could have, but I could remember well enough, and I was pretty certain the source had been right smack dab in the middle of the fifty-yard line.

As I hit the field, I got the faintest impression of another life. Looking over at those stands, for just a heartbeat I could imagine them being full of folks, cheering for me like I was some sort of star player. And maybe that could have been my life, at one point. But things had gotten away from me.

They always seem to do that.

I shook my head to drive away all those thoughts. I had a mission to complete, and then I could just ride off into the sunset or something. Maybe blow every cent on drugs and have the mother of all blowouts. Make Jimmy's jaw drop with the amount of money I dropped in his lap. Get something designer.

And so it was with visions of sugar plums dancing in my head that I came up on the center of it all. I couldn't see anything, not really, but faintly tickling around the edges of my hearing I thought I could hear the ocean.

Down in a Hole

I looked around but didn't see anything that could have been causing that sound. It was really faint, so much so that for a moment I thought that perhaps it was just the wind. But if I really focused on it, there it was. I could damn near feel the waves lapping around my toes, it was so real. I was pretty sure that my magical ability was why I was able to hear it; I had my doubts that anyone else would have. I mean, otherwise I would have liked to think I'd have heard about it, you know? Burgamy Village isn't so bustling a town that a football field that sounds like the ocean wouldn't draw a little conversation and gossip, if you catch my drift(wood).

With the lights off, the field was fairly dark. There was some moonlight shining down, but I wished I had a flashlight. I needed to do some hunting around, and my night vision wasn't all that great, what with my eyes being so red and tired. I rubbed them a bit and was a little surprised to find they were leaking a little.

A salty tear rolled down onto my upper lip, and I blinked with surprise. They weren't *tear* tears, if that makes sense. I was in full sad-sack mode, for sure, but I was also focused-ish on the task at hand, so it didn't make a whole lot of sense to me.

I wiped away the tears, then waited a minute to see if they would come back. When they didn't, I got down to business. Bending over, I started roaming around in a rough circle, one that I steadily worked bigger and bigger, looking for anything of note.

Of course, with there having just been a game, the ground was pretty torn up in a lot of places. The boys had really done a number in some spots, which made it hard to figure out what they had done versus what might have already been there. In the day I probably would have had better luck, but it was night, so there I was fumbling around like a blind man.

With a sigh, I got down on all fours. Crawling around like I had lost my glasses seemed the best move, and I hoped that patting around with my hands might help me out. Maybe by getting a little closer, something would catch my eye.

It took a good ten minutes, but finally I found something promising. There, amongst the grass and cleat-caused divots, was a small patch of dead grass. It could be and probably was nothing, but it was the only thing so far that had managed to stand out. And if memory and my ever-faulty drug-fueled senses served right, this was in about the exact spot I would have expected to find something, give or take twenty feet or so.

I sat there on my knees for a minute, wrangling in my mind the best way to go about this. There was probably zero risk in just digging down and seeing what sort of spell jar, husk, or wyrd stone might be down there. But . . . what if it wasn't any of those things? What if it was some sort of fuck-off weird creature? The kind that might nip my fingertips off if I went pawing around down there?

Futilely, I looked around to see if there was anything I could dig with instead of my hands. Of course, squatted down in almost the exact middle of a football field meant there was exactly nothing. I wasn't looking to spend all night here, so in the end my impatience got the better of me. I refused to walk my lazy ass over to the woods to find a stick or something. If I lost a finger . . . well, that would fit how the rest of this night was going.

The ground was warmer than I expected. I could feel a bit of heat radiating up through my palms, just enough that I could tell that something was going on. Moving my hand around to other spots within arm's reach, I could tell that the patch of dead ground was a good bit warmer than the rest. That just made me surer I was on the right trail.

I pulled at the grass, but it was short enough that I couldn't really get a good grip on it. At first I just started pawing at it like a dog but pretty quickly got tired of that. I don't have claws, and I ain't no mole. I thought about all the sticks and such I had seen earlier out on the tree line, then said, "Fuck it," and pulled off my belt.

My pants had been a "donation" from the back of the Christian Mission and were a couple sizes too big, so a belt had been required, and wouldn't you know it, there had been one of those in the drop box too. It had a big belt buckle—not like rodeo rider big, but large enough that it would be better than using my hands. It was some sort of steel, I reckoned, and had a big Alabama A on it, 'cause Roll fucking Tide.

Taking it in one hand, I started digging. The old cracked leather of the belt was course against my arm, but it mostly stayed out of my way, and while it was no shovel, it was better than using my damn fingers. I finally started to make some real headway, which was really breaking the mold on how my day had been going.

About six inches down, I heard the clank of metal on metal as the belt buckle hit something harder than dirt. I looked close, but it was too dark to really see anything. I set the belt aside and started working my fingers in the dirt, trying to get a feel for what I was working with. A brief inspection told me what it was.

It was the lid of a mason jar. Which meant that I was dealing with a spell jar. No doubt something of Granny's.

Fuck.

I could tell the lid was pretty rusted, most likely the product of age and having been buried in the soft, damp Alabama dirt. Carefully, I started working the dirt loose around it. I decided that I would dig the whole thing out; I didn't want to risk trying to pull it out half buried and end up cracking the glass. It was slow going, though, especially since I couldn't use the belt. I wasn't about to crack that glass just because I got into a rush. I stood a good enough chance of that happening just from being my usual unlucky self.

It took a little doing, but soon enough I had the damn thing free. It was still pretty well covered in dirt, so carefully I started to wipe the outside clean. I set it down on the ground and sort of rolled it across the grass, and that did the job well enough. There was a faint tinkling sound coming from within, from whatever Granny had tucked inside.

I got a glimpse of what I thought was bone, maybe a big tooth, and started to pull it up for a closer look, but that's when the voice came.

"If you know what's good for you, you'll put that back."

Hail Marshy

The voice was craggy, like rocks in a tumbler. A throat that had spent a lifetime yelling and smoking unfiltered cigarettes, from the sound of it. A coach's voice.

Looking up, I saw the Swampcats head coach standing there in all his far-too-in-shape-for-his-age glory. More troubling was the baseball bat he had slung over one shoulder. He wasn't being too menacing yet—I mean, it wasn't like he was swinging that thing at me—but there was a distinct ambiance of barely restrained violence to the situation. From my experiences in school, coaches rarely had the best tempers, and I was pretty sure that would go doubly for someone as old and muscly looking as him.

"Uh . . ." was the cutting remark I launched back at him.

The man took a step forward. I couldn't really see his face too well. He had on a ballcap, and while the moon wasn't in the right spot to shine a little light on him, I was certain the face wasn't smiling. "You heard me. That don't belong to you, so go-on-nah, put it back."

He said "go on now" like it was all one word, which told me all I needed to know about just how old-school backwoods this guy was. "Sorry, can't do it. I reckon you know that, though, especially if you know who I am."

"I don't reckon I do, on either account," he said, taking a step toward me and pulling that bat off his shoulder to start smacking repeatedly it into his empty palm. It was like we were in some cliché mafia movie, and I was the guy about to get kneecapped. "Put 'er back in the whole, and I won't have to whomp you one upside the head. Fair?"

"I'm a Marsh," I spat out. "You know. *Those* Marshes."

He shook his head slowly and took another step toward me. "I coached a couple Marsh boys at Sumpville over the years, but that don't mean shit now."

I wasn't really used to someone not knowing who I was, for good or (mostly) ill. I damn sure wasn't used to someone not at least cringing a little when they heard the Marsh name when magic was in the mix. So clearly this guy was either a better liar than me, or . . . he hadn't gotten this spell jar from Granny. Which could mean maybe someone else got it from her, then gave it to him, or maybe . . .

Fuck, it was too much to consider while staring down a bat-waving loon.

"Look, old man, I can't just let there be magic running wild like this. You got no idea what might happen." In fact, I could and routinely did let magic run wild just like this, and I also had no idea what might happen. The difference was that this time, I was being paid to care. "So I'm gonna dispose of this and no one will ever know the difference."

I could all but hear Coach's lip curl. "Magic? The hell you talkin' 'bout, son? What sorta drugs are you on?"

My jaw dropped. Did he seriously not know what this was? I shook the jar at him for a second before I realized what I was doing and stopped. "This. The spell jar. You know, a spell caught in a jar? The one that's been juicing up your team all season?"

"Don't you dare! Me and my boys aren't cheats!" He lunged forward at me, that bat not so much swinging at my head as poking toward my chest. As quickly as I could I scrambled to my feet, both hands on the jar so I wouldn't drop it. He kept coming closer, and I went to jump back.

And right as I started to do so, my pants fell down around my ankles, tripping me up and sending the jar sailing out of my hands. I think I let out a little shriek as it went flying, and I know for a fact I moaned when it hit the ground about ten feet away.

Even in the dark I could see that it had cracked.

Touchdown

The old man was still coming at me fast so I tried to scrabble away, all while trying to hitch up my pants. I had on some boxers, but it may surprise you to learn they *might* have had a few holes in them. The thought of this stranger seeing my bait and tackle as I tried to run away from him . . . well, it wasn't exactly a high point in my life. At this point, it was basically the shit cherry on this shit sundae of a night.

One hand on my pants, the other pushing me up as best it could, I managed to make my feet start working right in time to take a swift jump back to avoid getting jabbed in the sternum with the bat. I thought about trying to run around him and get my belt, but first I needed to avoid getting knocked out.

I had really struck a nerve—that much was clear. He was practically foaming at the mouth as he raged at me about cheating or something. Fuck if I was paying attention to the words, what with a bat coming at me! Needless to say I was rethinking a lot of my life choices right then.

Like the choice to not look at the jar. Ever know something bad was happening and decide to ignore it in hopes it would go away? That was me right then. Besides, I had plenty of bad right there in front of me. Heavy wooden bad.

For an old guy, he was faster than you'd have thought. He was less jabbing with that bat now and more waving it around. They weren't full swings, not yet, but sorta jerky halfway strokes like he couldn't decide just where he wanted to smack me yet. But the more he did it, the more he seemed intent on doing me some real harm.

The problem with your pants drooping is that even if you hold them up, if you don't pull them up enough, you end up stepping on the excess. And if the wrong foot steps on the wrong pant leg, you fall down. Don't ask me how I know this.

I landed on my ass with enough force to let me know my tailbone was gonna be good and bruised. But that was a minor concern, seeing as Coach seemed to have made up his mind. That bat came hurling toward me, right at head height. I managed to duck a little, but not enough, and it clipped the top of my skull.

My head rocked to the side and I tipped over sideways, falling over on the grass. I wanted to crawl away, but I couldn't do that *and* cover my head with my arms. I wasn't thinking clearly, and I couldn't believe that for the second time that night I was getting my ass whipped. Pants halfway down, in the middle of a goddamn football field, my downstairs bits very likely on display, as a man at least twice my age beat me down with a baseball bat. I've been fucking low, but damn, this was setting an all-time record.

I was shouting for him to stop, just begging, when another blow came down. This one hit my shoulder, and I promised whatever entity that was listening that I would go to church if nothing was broken, because the level of pain made me think there might be. Fight or flight was kicking in, and I tried to get away and cover myself all at the same time, doing a piss poor job of both.

And then the old dude stopped. It was like he realized just what he was doing, and the horror of it hit him all at once. He dropped that bat like it was some sort of poisonous snake and even took a step back. However, he dropped it on my shin, because of course he did—how else could this night go wrong?

He started stammering out an apology, eyes wide. Without a second thought I snatched the bat away from him. Holding it with one hand and cradling my battered head with the other, I managed to get my footing. Keeping my legs really wide apart kept my pants from totally falling down, though something was eventually gonna have to give: pants, bat, or injured head.

"I don't know what came over me . . ." he said as his eyes went wide. He wasn't looking at me anymore, instead looking kinda over my shoulder. I saw his jaw start to open and close, but no words were coming out.

I turned my head just a little. Too far and I would be seeing that jar, and I didn't want that. It wasn't real if I didn't see it, remember? But before I got my head shifted more than just a nudge, I could see a faint red glow that was gradually growing stronger. Swallowing the knot of fear that was lodged in my throat, I finished turning.

It took no time to realize that I couldn't see the jar anymore, though I knew it had to be there somewhere. Instead, a phantom tree was steadily growing into existence. It was already as tall as me, and with each passing second it grew at least a foot or more. Within a few heartbeats its dark red bows had spread overhead. It was the spirit of an oak tree, if I had to guess, and even through the hazy magic I could see it was knotty with age.

There comes a power with age, and I remembered Granddaddy telling me that things that lived over a hundred years had spirits that could be called on if you knew how. Had Granny found her a hundred-year-old tree and then jammed its spirit into a jar? Fuck if I knew. It didn't seem possible, but then what did I know?

The leaves were edged in a silvery sheen, and among the branches were glints of light like a spreading galaxy of stars. From the base of the trunk, roots began to grow their way out, and I could see they were a smaller mirror of the threads of power I had seen earlier. I took a step back as they neared my own feet, careful not to let them touch me.

The damn thing stopped growing when it was about fifteen feet tall, or at least it slowed to the point that it wasn't as noticeable. Because the larger it grew, the more one terrifying addition came into view. It was my turn for my eyes to get real wide as, behind me, I thought I heard Coach start to hightail it out of there.

Skewered on a broken limb was a hog, the limb jutting out from it like an extra leg. It had been stabbed in the side, and the spirit was dripping bright-red blood that was already forming a pool of crimson on the ground among the spreading roots of the oak. The roots nearest to the blood seemed to soak it up, growing darker as they did so. It was like the oak was using the hog's blood to grow its own power in some way.

This was a far darker magic than I was used to, and if it was from Granny like I thought . . .

Well, it didn't say much good about her, that's for sure.

I reached down deep for whatever remnant of power I might have in me. There was just the faintest trickle, a tiny nubbin that might have been enough to summon a spark to light a cigarette, but that was it. Most real wizards had been trained to tap into their own inner magic. Me, I could only tap into the tiniest trickle, and without drugs to burn for energy, I wasn't much more use than those goth kids in the woods.

Risking a glance back, I saw that Coach hadn't ran far. He'd gotten about forty feet away and stopped, though it was clear that he was prepared to take to sprinting at any second. I wished he would bring me my belt, and I almost asked him to—but before I could, I heard a crooning voice say my name.

"Hello again, Marsh."

It was the Hog of the Road.

And this time there was no protective circle between us.

Bacon Wrap

I turned my head back around, slowly, not wanting to actually see the damned thing. The demon—who, last time I saw it, had been trying to kill me—wasn't even looking in my direction. Instead it was sitting on the ground, gazing at the pig skewered there on the tree. Imagine a huge pink pig, only with jet-black eyes like a shark, two curling tusks, and the feeling of impending doom rolling off it in waves. That was what was looming there not ten feet from me, close enough that it could have those tusks buried in my gut in about two seconds.

"Hog of the Road," I replied with a calm that in no way mirrored what was going on inside me. I started jerking my hand backwards at Coach in the universal hand sign for "get the hell out of here." I couldn't risk looking away from the demon, and I wasn't about to start yelling at the man to run. If there was any chance that the Hog of the

Road hadn't noticed him, I'd be damned if I was gonna put the beast on his trail.

"Did you break the jar?" the demon asked. As it did, it lowered its head to sniff around the roots of the oak.

My first instinct was to lie—I mean, it usually is. But my gut told me that I wasn't gonna be able to lie my way out of this. I was pretty sure I wasn't gonna make it out of this one way or the other, so I figured I may as well go out being truthful for once. "Yeah."

I think it nodded. It was hard to say, really, because right about then it started to root its snout around the base of that tree. I hadn't tried to touch the tree, so I don't know if it would have been solid for me or just some sort of specter. But Hog, he managed to pass right through it as though it wasn't there. His face vanished for a moment as he slipped it into the trunk of the tree, then it came back out a few moments later.

As I watched, I thought I saw some leathery bit of flesh in its mouth. It looked like a pig's ear, I thought, though I only got to see it for a few seconds. The demon slowly chewed on it, and as he did, the pig impaled on the tree began to fade. By the time the Hog swallowed, the spectral pig had vanished, leaving nothing but a broken branch to show it had ever been there. Even the blood was gone, and the roots of the tree began to fade in color.

"You have done me a boon," the Hog said, still not looking at me. "So I won't kill you."

What do you say to that? I didn't have a clue, so in a real out-of-character moment for me, I kept my trap shut.

"She still has another piece of me. If you free the last as well, I will grant you a boon in return."

He could only be talking about Granny. Go against her like that? Not fucking likely. But I had to play the part. "Where is it?"

The Hog of the Road had gotten onto its trotters and was walking away from me. With each step, it started to fade. There were some metaphysics here I didn't have the foggiest clue about, but maybe HD could help me with that. All I really cared about was that it was going away.

"Hidden in a jar, where I can't find it."

And then the Hog was gone and I was left holding my pants, staring at an oak tree spirit that I didn't have the faintest clue what to do with.

Well That Was Anticlimactic

Without the hog's blood watering it, I guess the tree didn't have the oomph to survive on its own. In just a few minutes it had wilted away to nothing and blown away on some spectral wind or something. I don't know for sure, as I was spending that time handling a coach on the verge of a mental breakdown and finally putting on my belt.

I did learn about the origin of the spell jar, at least. Seems the good Coach Kersey, as I'd learned his name was, had been the assistant coach up at Sumpville for, like, decades. He'd been the number two guy to the legendary Coach Rawlings who'd taken the Lions to their decades of dominance. But when the old coach died, rather than give the head coach job to Kersey, the school had hired in some new guy. Pride being what it is, Kersey jumped ship to

Burgamy Village, where his wife was a teacher. And when he went, he took the "good luck charm" that Rawlings had buried on the fifty-yard line each season.

He had no idea where Rawlings had gotten it, and I didn't bother to give him the specifics. In truth, he didn't want to know, and I sure didn't blame him. The ways things went, I was pretty sure in a week or so he'd have made up some sort of story in his mind to square all this away in a non-magical way. Didn't much matter to me one way or the other. Not like anyone would believe him.

I did kinda feel bad for those boys, though. Their season was probably about to go to shit. Small as their team had been, they had all been getting *real* juiced. Now some team like Sumpville, with a fuck-off lot of players? It wouldn't have been nearly as notable, just enough to give them a little edge.

Anyway, once I got Kersey squared away back in his office in the field house, a small flask in his hand, I stepped back out onto the field. I gathered up the broken jar and its innards, thinking I should try and give it a good close study later when I got back to my shed.

I managed to find a nacho tray that had fallen under the stands to put it in. I had to scrape out the remnants of the cheese as best I could, but it would save me from getting cut on glass as I tried to carry it around. And then I settled down to wait in the parking lot in hopes that HD would be along shortly. I mean, it wasn't like I could call anyone. I decided if he didn't show in the next half hour or so, I'd take to trying to hitch home. Which, looking like I do . . . well, it wasn't the optimal plan. Let's just say that.

Sitting out there in the dark, just me with nothing to really distract myself with, gave me some admittedly unwanted time to kindly look inwards. What I saw was a complete mess. I was one small setback from having a total come-apart. And I mean *total*. I was in tears not long into the process, if I'm being honest. I should have felt better, all things considered. I mean, I had a big payday coming in soon, and I had managed to survive a run-in with the Hog. He'd even offered me a boon if I found another jar!

But what did that matter, really? I'd lost my girlfriend and just about my only friend, all in one night. I'd probably ruined some kids' season, just so some rich asshole could get his way. I'd almost been arrested and was banged up pretty damn bad.

I was feeling cored out, hollow, and what was filling me up was a whole lot of sad.

I think . . .

I think I've finally hit the bottom. And I knew that it was time to either dig up and out, or dig six feet deeper and be done with it. I had a choice to make, because I couldn't go on like this. I *wouldn't* go on like this.

Without my phone it was hard to tell the time, but when it felt like enough time had passed, I started to get to my feet. I guessed HD had abandoned me, too, and I didn't blame him. It was just the last nail in my eventual coffin. Feeling like I was, there was an equal chance I'd try to hitch out or just step in front of a semi barreling down the highway.

Headlights started to pan over me, and I shielded my eyes with my free hand. A car had pulled up into the parking lot, but with the lights like they were, I couldn't see who it was. Maybe it was Morgan come to finish me off. To put me out of my misery.

"I'm still mad at you," came Anna's angelic voice from behind the lights.

Jesus wept.

THE SWAMP KING

*Being the Eighth Tale in the Redemption of
Howard Marsh*

Black Dog

The massive black dog's jaws snapped at me, its huge teeth clamping shut in the air just shy of my arm. It lunged forward on back legs made of spectral wisps of shadow, but the fact that they weren't muscle and bone didn't slow it down any. He was *big* mad, and I happened to be closest at the moment.

"Anyone can make a spell jar, of course," Krista said from beside me, leaning in to take a closer look at the dog spirit she'd trapped inside some sort of fancy magic circle. "I mean, it's basically just throwing some crap in a jar, and then maybe you slip in a name on a scrap of paper. But if you want it to have real power—like capital-P power—you have to give it some source to draw on. Which can come from you, of course, if you don't care that its effect won't last really long."

I pointed to the Grim that was currently losing its goddamn mind a foot away from us. "But I'm betting it's better to let something else power it?"

Krista grinned. It turned out that she liked playing teacher, even if her only student was me. "Exactly! The trade-off, though, is you have to actually catch something to jam in there. Which isn't really easy, even if you've been trained as good as I have. 'Cause you can have all the skill in the world, but if you don't know where to find something good, it's pointless. So thanks again."

I'd been the one to find the Grim. I had, of course, played it off in my usual mysterious way—you know, letting on like I knew a lot more than I did, implying that I was secretly really plugged in good and well to the magical goings-on of the county. But really, it had been blind luck. The very old, very nice lady who lived a quarter mile from this little cemetery had hired me to find the other half of her dead grandmother's earrings and happened to mention seeing this "weird" dog when she went for "walkies" with her pet squirrel . . . which she had leash trained somehow.

Some folks are just fucking weird.

I reached down and scooped up my possum familiar, Horace, who was getting a hair too close to the magic circle. I grunted as I lifted him, holding his fat bulk against my chest. The Grim really started to go wild now, as if all he wanted in his unlife was to gobble down a drug addict spiced with a side of portly possum. I caught a good whiff of my pal, though, all sour milk and burnt grease, and set him back down a few feet away. That scent was gonna linger on my shirt, I just knew it.

"It can also be a lot more dangerous. I don't know if you've ever really looked at Granny's arms, but the old bitch is scarred up all over her arms from doing this."

I frowned. "Yeah, I don't get a lot of audiences with the queen, and I like to keep it that way."

Krista's frown matched mine. "Lucky. I wish she'd leave me alone like that."

My cousin had been dubbed the heir to our grandmother's legacy, very much against her will. They were a lot alike in some ways, like being stubborn beyond all reason, only Krista wasn't, you know, *evil*. Most times, Krista only had anything to do with the old bat if some sort of metaphorical gun was to her head. Right now, though, they'd come to some sort of truce, which near as I could tell meant that Krista would do some small things for Granny, and in return the Wicked Witch of the County would stop driving folks away from the salon my cousin had started.

I didn't want to keep thinking about Granny, so I sorta hunched down into a squat to get a closer look at the legs. I'd seen a few Grims over the years. They weren't common, exactly, but you visit enough graveyards and know how to look and you'll find one or two. For the most part, unless you were gonna die soon, they just left you alone. And even if they did see your death, all they did was walk alongside you for a spell, usually. Spectral good boys, so to speak—man's last best friend. Which, sadly, told me it was probably a good thing I had already gotten paid by Mrs. Neiman for finding that earring.

If you looked close, you could see that there were legs inside all that smoke and shadow, but they were skeletal. The bones were jet-black, though, which was why it was hard to see them until I got closer. It was weird as hell, but also kinda neat.

"Never seen a Grim get this pissed," I commented. "Usually they're just pretty chill, you know?"

"I guess he knows what's about to happen." Krista was digging out the mason jar from the Walmart bag she'd brought with her. She'd prepped it beforehand, so I didn't pay it any mind. I knew it held a Band-Aid, some seeds, a big acorn, some dirt from a fresh grave, and a dollop of honey.

"So how does it go from there"—I pointed to the glowing blue circle of sigils the Grim was battering itself against—"to that?" I asked, gesturing to the jar in her hand.

"Yeah, that's the tricky part. So basically, you put a small break in the binding circle with a silver nail so that the circle fades instead of just outright breaking. And then as it forces its way through, you use as much power as you can muster to compress it down and jam it in the jar. Then, while holding it in place, you clap on the lid and seal it with a sigil." She tapped the lid, where I could see a symbol drawn on in Sharpie. "Sigil's already done. Just gotta power it."

"You . . . compress it." I mean, I got what she was saying, but I hadn't the faintest idea of how you would even start trying to do such a thing.

Krista pulled a large silver nail from the pocket of her dress. "I know that sounds complicated, but it's not, re-ally. Basically you summon up your power and just . . . think it toward whatever you're trying to trap. And start thinking small thoughts at it. If you have enough power slamming into it, it'll be forced to shrink, then you shove it in the jar."

I looked at her blankly, trying to get the point across that she wasn't making a whole lot of sense. I mean, she was, but I was afraid if I acted like I understood it too well that she would make me try it. She was a big fan of the whole "learn by doing" bullshit, and I was feeling lazy.

"Look, it's not that hard. A Grim isn't all that power-ful. Just be careful you don't bite off more than you can chew"—she glanced at the slavering maw of the royally pissed off beast a foot away—"and you really can't mess this up. Look, how about you try it and see?"

And there it is.

"How about the fuck I don't?"

Krista grinned, holding up that nail. "I'd get ready, if I were you."

"Hold the fuck up—" I started, but she was already bending over. I lunged for the nail but she was too quick. With one fluid motion, she drug the nail right through one of the sigils. The blue light began to fade as the magic powering it dispersed.

The Grim went straight for the rapidly widening gap. Imagine a sheet of Cling Wrap and someone pressing their hand against it—that's what the dog's snout was doing, rather than bouncing off the boundary like it had been it before. Instead, it began pressing through, and I knew it was just seconds from breaking out.

I looked at Krista but she was already stepping back, damn near jogging backwards, really, in her rush to leave me holding the bag. To do this thing I had no fucking clue how to do. I wasn't even really all that hopped up on my usual bevy of illicit substances—not like I could have been had I known I'd be putting a Grim in a fucking jar! I was going to have to tap into Horace.

Reaching out, I connected to my familiar. He'd wandered off and was over by the cemetery fence line, rooting through some trash. He was still close enough, so I started calling upon the power I'd been stashing in him over the past week or so. I felt my possum pal freeze and knew if I looked over I'd see his hair all standing up on end. It didn't hurt, of course, but I knew he wasn't a big fan. It was too much like work for his tastes.

I felt that in a real way.

Scooping up the jar from the ground where Krista had left it, I put the lid in my left hand and the jar in my right. I didn't know what I was supposed to do with it, though, so I looked back at my cousin with what I am sure was a mighty pissed off look. She was making scooching motions with her hands, presumably telling me to get closer.

"Use your fucking words!" I shouted, turning back to the rapidly approaching catastrophe about to explode all over me.

"Jesus, don't overthink it! Just jam it in the jar!"

My voice started to get *reaaaal* high-pitched as the panic started to set in. I started jabbing the jar at the snout of the Grim, as if it would fit, shrieking the whole time. "*Howthefuckdoldothat?!*"

She made a grunting noise, and I was sure there were some sort of hand motions going on behind me, but I couldn't take the time to look. The snout of the hound had broken through the binding, and a splatter of spectral dog snot smacked my hand. It was hot and wet, and clearly real enough that I knew this dog's teeth would be just as real when they bit into my throat. I was going to haunt Krista so fucking hard.

The Grim shook its head from side to side, widening the hole with every passing second. It had its whole head out now and was working on its shoulders. I tried to stick the jar over its nose, but it was moving way too fast. And I wasn't about to try and grab it by the scruff; surely that was a recipe for losing a hand.

"What are you doing!? Magic, you fucking idiot, use your power! Force it down!"

I hadn't a damn clue how to "force it down," but I started sending out waves of magic toward it. It pulsed from my skin in a deep-green glow, flowing from my arms in a wave. Power without intent can't do anything; it just feels funny, like faint electricity. But I was thinking some real strong "get in the jar" thoughts, which I hoped would be enough.

I had to jump back as the Grim got its shoulders through. If the creature's back legs hadn't caught, it would have probably taken my hand off. As it was, I felt the hot breath coming from its mouth—that's how close it had been. I wanted to run, but I knew how that would end. I'm not a great runner on a good day, and there wasn't a dog alive that I could outrun, even without legs of spectral muscle.

I scraped up every ounce of will I could muster and focused it on the Grim. I visualized it getting smaller, slipping into the jar. Closing my eyes to focus harder was maybe the hardest thing I'd ever done, but really, I didn't want to see my death coming. With my eyes shut, I was able to really focus my will.

The snarling didn't let up. If anything, it redoubled, yet nothing sharp dug into my flesh, so I risked a glance. It was just a split second, but what I saw gave me a little hope, so I closed them again and tried to keep it going.

The Grim had stopped going for me, and in fact it looked like it was trying to go the opposite direction. Sure enough, its back half was steadily shrinking down and getting sucked into the jar. Those spooky legs were being stretched and turned into what looked like pure smoke, like a genie coming out of a lamp in reverse. I would have laughed if I hadn't been so focused.

It took about thirty seconds, but the snarling started to get real squeaky. Opening my eyes, I saw the head was finally starting to shrink down and get sucked into the whirlpool of the spell jar. I almost felt bad for the damn thing at that point. The look on its face was one of surprise more than anger, and the snarls had mostly turned into squeaky yips.

"Now put the lid on it!" Krista shouted. She had gotten a lot closer, maybe a couple feet behind me now from the sounds of things.

The head had all but vanished, so I moved to place the lid over the mouth of the jar. I wasn't all that surprised to find that my hand was shaking, so I didn't get a snug fit on my first try. As I started to try again, I felt the Grim nip my thumb with its now tiny teeth. I swore as a little spurt of blood shot out; the damn thing had gotten me good. Worse, it was enough to cause my focus to slip.

The Grim started to reverse course, its head growing larger once more. The panic started to return, and that helped things, uh, not at all. The power I had wasn't limitless, and I was gonna be running on fumes here real quick. Horace was about tapped out, and without his strength to draw on, I was proper fucked. I started cussing up a blue streak

I was about to lose all control, but then I felt a wave of power join my own. The dark green of my magic blended with a pale yellow as Krista stepped in to take control. A heartbeat later, the Grim was tucked away, totally shrunken and turned to a cloud of black smoke within the heart of the glass.

This time I got the lid on right, slamming it on quickly and firmly, then Krista sent a pulse of her power into the lid, sealing it up nice and tight. Looking in the jar, the smoke had vanished. I could see a faint haze, but one so thin that I doubted anyone who lacked power would be able to even get a hint of it.

Krista took the jar from me. "See? Easy."

Raise Hell, Praise Dale

I didn't have a clue when or why the opening race of the dirt track season became the day that those who could use power in the county came together, but as long as I could remember that had been the case, and I had never made the guest list. Which was fair, and that was actually how I liked it. Most anyone with power I had ever met, I'd gotten on their bad side.

Though, if I was being real honest with myself, that went for pretty much anyone, power or not.

Krista had insisted that since she had spent the morning "teaching" me how to craft a spell jar like I had asked, I now owed her. I argued that tossing a kid into a river filled with snakes and shouting "Swim!" wasn't teaching, and that was pretty much what she had done to me. We'd have agreed to disagree except for the fact that she was my ride. So unless I wanted to start hitching from the back ass of nowhere, I was stuck going along on the ride.

A ride that entailed us coming out to Ward Peebles Speedway for the annual confab of magic users. It was her first ever also, seeing as she'd been tapped by Granny to be the family representative this year. Once I learned the old bat wasn't going to be there, I was a little more on board. I'm no car nut, not by a long stretch, but dirt track races could be fun to watch.

To see them, though, we would've had to actually have gone into the speedway. Instead, we were hanging out in the shadowy outskirts of the field that doubled as a parking lot. There had to be at least two hundred cars parked all around, mostly just lumps of darker color amongst the shadows. No one had invested any money in lighting the parking lot, which, judging from the supernova glow of lights coming from inside the speedway, was because there hadn't been any bulbs left.

Krista had done us a solid and scooped up a mess of Natty Daddys on the way. I'd already crushed two and was starting to feel alright. The glares my cousin cut me as I cracked open number three made me feel even better.

"Don't you dare get drunk," she hissed at me.

I locked eyes and took a looong pointed sip. The burp after was a little forced, but the huff it got outta her was giving me life. Besides, she was on number two herself, and she'd definitely smoked her fair share of the joint I'd brought. She was gonna be feeling real alright herself if she wasn't careful.

It was probably nerves, I realized. Krista was a Marsh, so she could hold her own when it came to powering through a shitload of beer. But she was also really responsible—disgustingly so—so I knew she wouldn't have had that many if she wasn't trying to calm her nerves on down. I wasn't sure what went on at these meetings, and the vibe I was getting from her was that she didn't really know either. Granny was also a big fan of "sink or swim" teaching.

Makes you wonder where Krista got it from.

Before we could get good and going on the squabbling, Preach showed up. He was about as big as the two of us put together, just big slabs of meat hanging on a fuck-off big frame, and had that sort of always frowning face that made you think his mom had just died. Preach was wiping at his shaved head with a small blue towel that he had hanging from around his neck. When he saw me standing there, his frown somehow managed to deepen.

"Granny Marsh just trying to tick folks off, now, sending you?"

I wanted to flip him a bird, but he was still real mad at me for burning down his butcher shed. That, and foiling his attempt to feed a demon hog to his customers to save on the cost of pork. So, I just gestured to Krista. "She's the one that's here. I'm just tagging along for the ride."

Preach nodded to Krista. "I'm sorry."

Krista reached out and shook his hand. Preach could have damn near palmed her whole forearm, such was the size difference. "Thanks. I'm regretting it already."

A thought came to me then. "Preach, you went to Burgamy Village, didn't you?"

The big man turned back to look at me. He didn't say anything at first, but his eyes narrowed a bit as he gave a slight nod. "Why?" he asked, a clearly unwarranted amount of suspicion in his voice.

"You ever go to the football games? Heard they had a good year last year." It had been a great year until I got involved, actually. They ended up losing to Sumpville but still managed to make the 1A playoffs, though they didn't make it past the second round. Still, only losing two games on a season? Well, anyone would be happy with that, I reckoned.

"I work for a livin', Marsh. Ain't got time for such foolishness. 'Specially as business is harder than it needs to be right now," he answered pointedly.

"That's my point, though. I went to one of their games, and the food fuckin' sucks. You went to school there—why don't you try to become the new food guy instead of whatever idiot is running Manky Hotdogs 'R' Us? Folks would rather eat pulled pork than peckers and lips disguised as a hotdog any day."

"I wouldn't even know who to talk to," he said, trying to blow off my idea like it was bad. I make bad choices—like, every waking moment—but I'm not *dumb*. I mean, not really. Ok, I am an idiot, but even a blind squirrel finds a nut sometimes. I knew this idea was a good one, and I could see just as clearly that Preach had some gears turning in the big bald head of his.

Then Morgan came up, her arm entwined with some hairy motherfucker that looked like the love child of a Sasquatch and a biker.

I kinda wanted to run, as Morgan was nuttier than a run-over road lizard and had maybe tried to kill me once, but I was honestly too entranced by the walking shag carpet beside her. I had to know who the hell he was, if for no other reason than I wanted to ask Uncle HD later who had fucked a sheepdog to spawn this bastard.

I mean, he was *hairy*. I worry that I am underselling that fact. You could have braided this guy's arm hair, if you could even find his arms behind the gray-black beard that damn near covered all of his chest. His head hair was long, too, and looked like it had once heard a rumor about a comb but didn't consort with such foolishness.

"Preach, you look as happy as ever," Morgan chirped, freeing herself from Cousin It to wrap her arms around Preach in a hug.

I swear he almost smiled for a second. Instead, he just looked a little less dour as he hugged her back. "Morgan! Didn't know you was back."

Krista had stiffened slightly beside me, and I looked her way. She'd plastered on her pageant face, complete with a huge smile that didn't come close to reaching her eyes. I knew her well enough to know that in that moment, she was wishing she had something stronger than beer to drink. Morgan had only kidnapped me because she hadn't known at the time that Krista was the heir apparent. When Morgan had been run outta town, Granddaddy was still alive, and I'd been his favorite. So Krista had been made well aware that the woman who'd come back to kill Granny would likely also be a danger to her. And here she was.

"Morgan, it's so good to see you again," Krista said as soon as the hug was over. Her voice was sickly sweet, that kind of catty that made it ever so clear that while the words were nice, there was no love lost.

"Oh, always," Morgan replied, matching her tone. She motioned to the man beside her. "I believe you know Knut."

"Only by reputation, of course," Krista said. "Granny has always told me of the prowess of your family, Mr. Knut."

"Just Knut," growled the hairball. His voice was like a gravel truck that had spent decades smoking three packs a day. I didn't think he was trying to be unfriendly; I thought maybe that was just how his voice was. Handshakes started being passed around—none of them coming my way, mind you, but I figured it was getting close to time for me to fade away anyway. I had no business being here, and folks were making that damn clear.

I was about to walk off when Morgan decided to rain on my parade. "Howie, I was telling Knut here about how I saw you at that football game on the way over here."

This time Knut really did growl.

Knowing the difference now, I can safely say that when the man is pissed, he's not afraid to show it. A scowl like a thunderstorm peeked out from behind that face full of fur and he jabbed a thick finger in my direction. "Keep the fuck out the village. You're just lucky she found you, instead of me or one of my boys."

A wiser man would have just nodded and apologized. But I wasn't even supposed to be there, I wasn't wanted, and above all: fuck 'em. "Are your boys as hairy as you? Or do they take after someone more human? Just asking, so I know if I need to keep a set of shears on me."

In the slack-jawed silence of Knut's shock, I faintly heard Krista mutter a quick "Goddamn it."

All in all, I didn't expect Preach to get in between me and Knut, but I am really damn glad he did. The hairball managed to get in a glancing blow on my right ear even from around Preach's side, but that was about it. It gave me the freedom to keep shouting insults at the berserker carpet as Krista tried to pull me away.

And of course, Morgan was just cackling away like it was the funniest thing she'd ever seen. Which didn't seem to do anything to calm down ol' Knut, who shouted at her to "shut her damn trap" between the curses he was raining down on me. That was somehow even funnier to Morgan, who was hunched over with laughter at this point.

Krista ended up grabbing me by the ear, which fucking hurt and was totally uncalled for. Dragging me by the ear, she pulled me off away from the shouting, then gave me a little slap and shove into the nearest car. It wasn't enough to hurt, other than the ear pulling, but it did sting a little.

"Why are you like this?!" Krista shouted at me. "Just behave for once in your fucking life, goddamn it!"

I jabbed angrily in the direction of where it all began. "He started it! I didn't even do anything and he started threatening me. I don't even know who the hell he is!"

"I told you this, jackass, on the ride over, but of course you weren't paying me any attention," she seethed. She ran her hand across her face, as if trying to wipe the image of my face from her mind. Breathing deep, she didn't open her eyes. "You know what, I should have known better. This is on me. I should have known better than to think you could manage to act right, even for me, for two seconds."

That stung. Yeah, she'd talked about the folks who were going to be at this meeting, but I'd been rolling a joint—and didn't want to be there anyway, so I made no effort to listen. But she had to see that I didn't start this. I started to protest, but she slashed her hand through the air to cut me off, even though, near as I could tell, her eyes were shut.

"I'm going to count to ten to calm down. And when I hit ten, I am going to open my eyes, and you are not going to be here. Because if you are still where I can see you, you will regret it. So go watch the races, buy a beer—I don't care, but do it far from here. I'll come get you when the grown-ups are done."

"Krista . . ."

Again with the slashy motion. "Don't 'Krista' me. One . . . two . . . three . . ."

I threw my hands up. "Fuck it."

If she got to ten, I couldn't tell you, because I was long gone by then.

Wheeler Dealer

T hey charge at the door to get in to see the races, of course, and I was way too pissed off to waste money on watching some folks take a bunch of left turns. I'd also promised Anna that I was going to start taking better care of my finances as part of her taking me back, which I was almost . . . mostly . . . doing. So, I was resigned to waiting in the parking lot, at least on the far side away from where Krista and what looked like closer to a dozen folks were now having a little confab.

But then I saw Johnny and Emily getting out of their van.

Johnny had his fiddle, and the two of them were dressed in their Sunday best, so it was pretty clear to me that they were performing. Ever a shrewd wheeler and dealer, I figured I'd see if they needed someone to carry their gear for them, in exchange for being "part of the band," at least long enough to get into where they had beer for sale.

They at least were excited to see me as I came up out of the pale yellow light of the parking lot toward where they were unloading a few things. "Marsh!" they cried out damn near in unison, and Emily even gave me a big hug. When an angel like Emily hugs you, you just count yourself lucky and shake off whatever's been keeping you down.

Their smiles were infectious, and within seconds I was grinning like a jackass as I shook Johnny's calloused hand in mine. "Evening, y'all," I said. "Got a show tonight?"

"National anthem," Johnny said.

Emily nodded, then looked over toward the race track. "We're a little late. They haven't started yet, have they?"

"We can hear each other talking, so I don't reckon so," I answered with a wink. Dirt track racing was fucking loud, and once they got up and going you'd be able to hear things many miles away.

Johnny smiled at his wife. "They won't start until the anthem, and since that's us . . ."

"Y'all need a hand?" I asked.

"You are such a saint, you know that?" Emily beamed, handing me a bag that held some cables and micro-phones. "We probably won't need half this stuff, but better to have it and not need it than need it and not have it, you know?"

"You right," I said, grabbing a pair of microphones stands in my other hand. "Just consider me your roadie for the night."

And that's how I got inside for free for only a couple minutes of work.

An hour later we were back out by their van, splitting a jar of 'shine that Johnny had gotten as a tip from an appreciative racer. I'd never heard "The Star-Spangled Banner" played on a fiddle before, but it had been pretty alright. I was pretty convinced that those two couldn't make bad music if they tried; even a wrong note would probably sound like art with the skill they had. Naturally, the crowd had eaten it right up.

Only Johnny and I were sipping, Emily having resolved to drive, she said. But it was nice to just linger and drink, catching up on things. Only once had I been able to get out to the Camp where they lived since all that bullshit with Morgan and that poor girl she'd killed. I'd tried to find that redcap that I thought had to be running loose around there, but no dice. Damn thing was either better at hiding than I'd ever known one to be, or it had moved on.

So, I'd just let it be. I sorta felt like me showing up there a bunch wouldn't be the most welcome of things anyway. Guys like me, we wear out our welcome pretty damn quick. And besides, I was a memory of a bad time. The Camp had a reputation as a hippie-dippie happy place, and Kandra's death was a dark stain on that. Me showing my face, well, that would just bring up bad memories. There ain't enough places like the Camp in the world, so I wasn't about to ruin that one by overstaying my welcome.

But damn if talking with them didn't make me realize how lonely I'd been lately. Liam had yet to forgive me after the football game debacle, HD had been busy working, Lida was all caught up in her new guy, and even Corey, my neighbor in the storage units, was spending more and more nights elsewhere. If Anna and I hadn't worked things out, I'd have been stuck with just Krista, and I think it's pretty clear that we have limits on how long we can be around each other.

Anna was good for me, I knew that much. She was slowly helping me get better, be better. I mean, sure, the changes were pretty damn miniscule, but still. The flip side of that, though, was that I wasn't as comfortable hanging out with the worst of the reprobates I used to hang out with. And with my halfway decent folks all caught up in their own lives, and Anna being in school during the week . . . well, it made for some lonely days. But when you've been so down for so long, it can be hard to notice just what's making your mood bottom out.

I was happier than I had any right to be. Again, I knew that much, but I was still lonely. And actually practicing my magic like I should have been this whole time was a poor substitute for the company of real live people. I'd missed just hanging out like this in ways I hadn't realized until I was in the middle of it.

All this is to say that when they ended up inviting me out to the Camp to spend some time with them, my first instinct was to refuse like I had pretty much every other time recently. But, after a few moments of thought, I decided that I would take them up on that. Not this weekend; it was too last-minute, and I didn't want to miss out on even more of my weekend with Anna by disappearing into the swamp. But I asked if I could come out one day that upcoming week, and they seemed to genuinely love the idea. So with plans made, they decided to head on home, and I couldn't much blame them.

Watching their taillights vanish in the distant dark would have been a lot sadder if I hadn't had something to look forward to now. So, with my mood brighter than it had been in a long time, I wandered back to Krista's car, climbed into the back seat, rolled up a fat joint, and woke up Horace from his nap so I could play with him.

Things weren't great, but you know, sometimes life wasn't half bad.

No Good Deed

I was holding the Grim-filled spell jar carefully in between my legs. Krista didn't know I had stolen it; at least she hadn't when she'd dropped me off at my shed last night. Judging from the several missed calls I had from her on my phone, well, I suspected she had come to realize it wasn't where she had left it. In my defense, I had pretty much done everything that mattered except buy an empty mason jar. So really, it should have been mine to begin with.

Besides, she was just going to give it to Granny, who would probably use it to be the shit in someone's corn-flakes. Now me? I had a much better use for it. Even Anna had agreed, though I had decided to leave out the details of just who technically owned the jar. I could also tell she didn't really believe in the power of the jar, but I couldn't really blame her there. She was giving me a ride and humoring me. What more could I really want?

I tapped the glass and got a faint impression of snarling dog teeth. It was almost certainly just my imagination; a sealed spell jar means that nothing at all can get out, but it felt real enough. So much so, in fact, that I decided to stop playing with fire and tapping on that glass. Instead, I reached over and took Anna's hand in mine. Her long fingers entwined in mine, and I could feel the cool metal of her rings against my own.

She looked over at me and smiled, then looked back to the road, the ghost of the smile lingering long on her lips after. We had the windows down, so her long blonde hair was whipping around a fair bit. My own hair was getting shaggy, enough that it was sort of flicking around the edges of my vision, but that was how I liked it. The breeze felt nice, and we both had on our shades to mind the sun. Anna's were these cute rose gold and pink glasses with points on the corners like cat ears. It made her fucking adorable, not that she needed it. Mine came from—you guessed it—the donation box out behind the Christian Mission, black and scratched up to hell and back.

It was a typical Alabama March morning. Right now it felt nice and springlike, and the forecast called for it to get hot as balls in the afternoon. Three days ago we had a freeze warning, and there was every chance in the world that we would get another later in the week. If you don't like the season in March, don't worry; it'll go from spring to winter to summer and back again every couple of days.

But right then, it felt fucking amazing coming through the windows.

It was almost a shame when she pulled into the Jackson Hollow One Stop. I could have happily rode like that forever. 'Course, I was pretty damn high, so that helped, but a long ride with only the whipping wind for a soundtrack isn't a bad way to spend a morning.

"Need anything? Coke or a snack?" I asked her, hand on the door.

"Yeah, anything. Thanks." She had pulled a brush out of the glove box and was starting to run it through her hair. She wasn't as uptight about her hair as some of the women I'd dated, but she was particular about it not getting too tangled.

From the floorboard I scooped up a small brown paper sack and slipped the jar inside. Then I started heading for the store. There was an old green Ford Ranger with a bewildering number of dents and dings pulled up to the pump. Some young'un I didn't recognize who couldn't have been more than seventeen or eighteen was there, dip cup in one hand, pump handle in the other. He nodded my way and sent a dribble of brown spit into the cup, poorly, getting almost as much in the scraggly goatee he was trying to grow. I didn't bother nodding back.

One thing I liked about Terry and Emma, the owners of the One Stop, was that they weren't churchgoers. I don't really care what people do so long as it doesn't affect me, but most of the gas stations in the parts of the county I tended to find myself in would close at least Sunday mornings, if not the whole day. Having one you knew was always open to get some smokes from if you needed them was nice.

Stepping inside, I pulled my sunglasses off with my free hand, folding them up and slipping them onto the neck of my tank top. Emma was there behind the counter, hunched over, reading a book she was already setting down. "Howard Marsh, it's been awhile!"

I smiled and gave a little wave. "Has, at that. You know how it is."

She looked out the window that looked onto the lot. "Sure do. Who's that pretty young thing in the car out there?"

Laughing, I started walking around, scooping up some drinks and snacks. Diet Dr. Pepper for Anna, Coke for me, with some Hot Fries and a Twix for us both to munch on. Emma and I made small talk the whole time. She was a bit of a gossip, but then so was I whenever folks deigned to tell me the juicy stuff.

Items in hand, I got to the register, giving Emma a good hard look for the first time as she totaled up all the items by memory. She had lost some weight, and her face had more lines than ever. Her husband Terry's cancer was taking a toll, that was clear, even if she was trying to do her best to hide it.

"Eight twenty-three should do it," she said a few seconds later.

I did not have $8.23. I had four ones in my wallet, and maybe another dollar in small change in the pocket of my shorts. But cash had never been the plan here. I pulled the jar from the sack and set it on the counter. "That should cover it, I reckon."

Her eyes narrowed in confusion for a second, then grew wide. "Is that . . ." she whispered, her hand reaching out tentatively, as if moving too quickly might scare the jar away.

"It is. Bury it wherever he spends the most time, at night. Or if y'all have a cemetery plot, put it there. Just dig the hole under a full moon, and make sure that moonlight hits it good and plenty before you cover it up."

She picked it up carefully, staring into the detritus that partially filled it. "Will it . . . cure him?"

Sadly, it wouldn't. I was sure there might be magic that could cure cancer as bad as what was eating Terry Jackson from the lungs out, but I didn't know it. But bottling up a Grim like that—it would work to hold off death for a good long while. Maybe long enough for the doctors up in Montgomery to work their own kind of magic. So I shook my head. "It'll slow things down, though. Give you a lot more time."

She started to cry, and she got up off the stool she'd been sitting on and damn near ran around the counter to wrap me up in a hug. She was about as short as I was, so I could feel her wet tears on my shoulder, but I didn't much mind.

I might have shed a tear or two, but that was probably just from how tight she was squeezing me. In the end she offered me a lot more than $8.23 in snacks, damn near racing to open up the cash register. And Granny? She'd have charged a whole lot of money for that jar. Couple thousand, easy. It was probably why the old witch hadn't done this herself.

But I ain't her.

$8.23 was good enough for a friend, I reckoned.

Besides, how could Krista be mad at me now?

SHARP POINTY TEETH

"I'm surprised you even remember Granddaddy brought you out here," Krista said.

She'd forgiven me, mostly, when she found out just what I had done with the jar. That is, on the condition that I was going to make it up to her at some point in the future. I mean, I had absolutely no intention of doing so, but she had her ways, just as I had mine. We'd see how it'd play out.

For now, though, she was doing me a small favor and giving me a little lift out to the Camp on her way to Troy. And for a share of a joint, I was able to convince her to stop at this little road cut that was one of my absolute favorite places on the planet. She was right; I knew it from Granddaddy bringing me here when I wasn't but five or so.

There ain't a straight road in Jubal County that I know of. All the paved roads used to be dirt roads. Go back far enough and you'll see that it was horses and wagons and shit that made them for the most part, and by and large they followed the path of least resistance, going around hills where they could, that sort of thing. But as technology came along, it became a much easier thing to cut right into a hill and bridge two points.

At some point before I was born, the powers that be decided that it was time to widen out Freeman Road to two lanes, and while they were at it, they were gonna straighten it out a little. And so in a few places they basically cut away the side of a few hills, leaving places like what lay before us.

Krista had parked the car on the grass on the side of the road. About ten feet from the driver's side door, a red dirt bank that looked like it had been sheared rose up about forty feet high. Maybe more—I'm kinda shit with distance. The base of it had a tumble of soft rocky clumps among a dense weave of thorny underbrush. About head height on up till almost the top, it was mostly smooth dirt, so flat that nothing was able to grow there, leaving it open to the elements. And then as you kept looking up, you began to see the roots of some of the trees lining the top, keeping the whole place from just washing away in the next hard rain.

It was those rocky bits at the bottom that drew me here.

See, millions of years ago, Montgomery was beachfront property. And Jubal County, it had all been underwater. Go deep enough and you can find the proof of it. But if you're like me, there's no need to dig if you can just find a spot like this where the deep parts of the earth have been made into the surface.

"Been coming here for years and years. Granddaddy got me hooked," I said, hunched over a lump of chalky stone about the size of my chest. Life took a bad turn for me, but I think in a different world, a different life, I'd have been a paleontologist. 'Cause there were few things in life I loved more than coming here and diggin' in the dirt to find the past.

It was soft enough that I was able to break up chunks of it with my hands. It wasn't stone, of course, but it was more than just dirt, so it held together really well until put under some pressure. Maybe that's why I liked this so much; I saw a lot of myself in it.

I'd only been there a couple minutes, but already I'd found a couple of nice old shells about the size of my fist. I wasn't gonna keep those. They were so common that it wasn't worth it after the first dozen or so I'd found as a much younger kid. But I'd also found a tiny coral tube, which was a much harder find. That I sat to the side, careful not to break it, even though it wasn't the reason why I was here.

No, I was searching for teeth.

'Cause where there's oceans, there's always sharks. And has been for millions of fucking years. Hard to improve on perfection when it comes to apex predators, so if you hunted here long enough, you could always find at least a fragment of a shark tooth. And if you were lucky, like I was hoping to be, you could find some really badass ones.

In theory, I could have just grabbed some of the one I had already found. I had a coffee cup full of them back in my shed, one of the few bits of flotsam and jetsam in my life that had always managed to hang around. I didn't know what it might be worth and had, in fact, made a point to never try to find out. Ain't a lot that was special to me in my life at this point, and if I ever sold them off for a fix, well, then that'd be it for me.

I really wanted to find a megalodon tooth. That was my white whale: a shark tooth bigger than my fist. If I could ever clap hands on one of them, I could die happy. But here in this road cut, I had never found anything bigger than about the size of my thumbnail. Most were about half a finger joint long and nail thin. Hell, most were actually just fragments. I'd actually found one of them already, a speck of almost black about as big as a grain of rice. But for what I was thinking, I wanted some whole teeth. And I damn sure wasn't going to be giving away some from my own stash.

My already dirty nails were getting even worse as I used my fingers to pry apart the rocks on my quest for toothy gold. I could hear Krista behind me starting to huff, though, and I knew my time was likely growing short. I didn't bother rushing, however. Some things you can't just race through.

I heard the keys jingle. "You said it would be a quick stop."

"Yep," I replied, tossing another nice shell to the side. I had an idea that maybe I could start collecting those, maybe set up at a yard sale or something. Surely someone would pay a couple bucks for them, right? I didn't have room in the little backpack I had brought along, though, so that was a project for another day.

"Yep," she mimicked in a voice that sounded absolutely nothing like mine. I wasn't looking, but I'd bet she was making a face and some hand motions to go with it.

I just kept my head down, not rising to the bait. That's when a mini miracle happened—clearly some good karma for not getting deservedly mouthy with my impatient cousin. Popping open a bit of rock, there were three almost perfect teeth right in a row. I'd never in my life found even *two* teeth side by side like that, and the sight of it sorta caused my breath to catch. I'd have to gently break away the dirt around them, but in one fell swoop I had found exactly what I was here for.

"Look, I got places—" Krista had started, but I was already turned around and headed for the car, breaking off the bulk of the unneeded rock as I did.

"You gonna just stand there all day, or are we gonna hit the road? Some folks got places to be, ya know."

I swear to God, that stutter she loosed as her brain fried a little—it made my whole damn week.

ONE LONE NIGHT

The Camp sure was emptier these days, which might have been a little sad had I liked people more. Time was, a nudge more than a dozen folks had called it home but now it was half that, what with a bunch of folks moving off after Kandra had died. At least I had my pick of places to stay, really, as no one had bothered to take their tarps and hammocks when they left.

After everyone else had gone to bed around ten, Johnny and I stayed up until at least two in the morning, I reckoned, sipping and toking, nothing too crazy. Ever stay up all night just talking with someone around a small fire, just staring at the coals as they bathe you both in a pale red light? There's a sort of magic there that has nothing to do with power, something primal, and it was just what I'd been needing without realizing it. Hell, we solved all the world's problems in that talk, if only folks had been around to listen.

They were real judgment-free here in the Camp, so he even let me indulge in the harder stuff without making a fuss, which meant I wasn't really running on much in the way of sleep. I'd more or less sort of paced around once Johnny went to bed till it was getting close to dawn, then I crawled into the hammock they'd offered me to sleep in. Not that I slept, really. I mostly just fidgeted and tried to figure out if the weird noises I was hearing were a product of the drugs or something to be concerned about.

I mean, I was too high to actually be concerned about much, but the noises certainly were intriguing as all hell. If I'd had better night vision, or knew where a flashlight was, I might have just tore off out into the brush to see just what in the hell was prowling around out there. But—probably for the best, as I wasn't thinking all that clearly—I ended up just lying there listening.

At first, all I noticed were the droning sounds of crickets and cicadas. They were a constant noise, more comforting than anything, as I'd been hearing them all my life. Throughout, I could hear frogs and such going off, a couple of different types. I'm no frogologist, though, so I couldn't begin to tell you what types they were, 'least not from sound. One kind had a sort of deeper croak, while another was more of a higher-pitched trill. Neat, but nothing I hadn't heard a million times before. Just a bit louder than normal because swamps are frog central, I reckoned.

But then I started to hear things that were . . . less normal.

Things like a twenty second peal of laughter, only real faint and distant. So much so that I was certain that it wasn't coming from anywhere in the Camp, especially given that everyone but me was asleep. It also sounded off, like whatever was laughing didn't have the same kind of throat a human would. It was like someone had once heard laughter years ago and was trying to recreate that noise from memory, but the memories were all sad ones, dripping with such sorrow that it came through in the laughter.

I don't know why, but the moment I heard it, I got this vision in my mind from this book I read as a kid: *Scary Stories to Tell in the Dark*. It had all these super fucked up pictures in it—like really messed up stuff that should never have been in a book for kids. There was this one drawing I remember of a sad-eyed horse with a super long face. It would have been comically long if not for the twisted body that held it up, all misshapen limbs and dingy fur. Something about that laughter made me think of that picture. It was bizarre and sorrowful, like the morose eyes of that horse.

It rang out twice, about five minutes apart from each other. I think it was a little closer the second time, but other than that it was identical in sound. Same rise and fall, same inflection. It could have been a recording, it was so similar. Hell, it may have been, though why someone would be wandering through a swamp playing recordings like that, I couldn't begin to fathom.

And let's be real, it could have been the drugs. I didn't think it was, but really there was no way to be sure.

What I was slightly more sure about was the bustle in the hedgerow. And by that, I mean I heard some shit moving around in the bushes near the Camp. Which isn't uncommon, of course, seeing as there are all sorts of wild critters that call the county home, but live here long enough and you get a feel for what goes on four legs and what goes on two. Whatever was lurking was on two legs. And I was like almost certain I heard the sound of that thing taking a piss on the side of the camper that Johnny and Emily slept in.

That almost got me up, not gonna lie. I was pretty dead set on it. I mean, no one disrespects my hosts like that—not on my watch! But then I heard the sound of a blade getting sharpened and decided that life was pretty good in my hammock. No point in getting caught up in shit that didn't involve me, you know?

There is something absolutely terrifying about the sound of a hone scraping down the length of an unseen blade. It being pitch-black only made it worse. The only good thing was that as long as I could hear that grating sound, I knew how close it was to me. But suddenly I couldn't hear it anymore, and I knew that something was walking around in the dark with a sharp weapon. Something creeping around, maybe passing right beside my hammock. Maybe slipping under it. Maybe getting ready to slip that weapon through the thin material of the hammock and into my defenseless back.

I was pretty well frozen with fear. I crossed my fingers that they would trip and land on the blade. Would serve them right for being fucking creepy in the woods at night.

But nothing happened. I thought I heard a few more steps, and then things were quiet again except for the crickets and frogs. I listened hard, but all I could hear was my heart thudding away from a combination of drug strain and terror.

So I lay there, too afraid to move, at least until I managed to almost convince myself that it was all just the fault of the drugs. That nothing had been moving through the Camp with lethal intent, pissing on campers. And so there I lay until I heard folks start to wake up and start moving around, about thirty minutes later.

The scent of coffee is what really ended up luring me out from my cocoon. If I was gonna die, I was gonna go out caffeinated. The faces that greeted me had no hints of fear lingering in their eyes, and if anyone else had heard the same fuckery I did, they didn't talk about it over the strong black brew that Emily was doling out like a priest giving sacrament. It certainly saved my soul.

Most times you get some sleep, so you never feel the hangover coming. You just go to bed happy and drunk, then wake up feeling like hammered ass. But the little cocktail of oblivion I had taken, coupled with terror, had kept me from sleep, so I'd been awake for every second of the hangover blossoming within me. It wasn't a great feeling, to be honest. I definitely had some mild regrets. But that coffee, I was pretty sure, would fix me right up.

At least once I got done throwing up. It was only a little, though. Like I said . . . it wasn't a bad hangover.

Time I Collect My Bones

The patch of land the Camp called home was about as pretty a swamp as a boy could ask for. So much so that once the coffee had helped me shake the worst of the hangover, I decided to indulge my love and go for a bit of a walk about. I didn't get to go roaming off through my favorite terrain all that often, and by God, I was gonna make the most of it.

I don't know when it was exactly that swamps became my favorite place on earth, but that had certainly been the case in recent years. Maybe it came from growing up in the county. See, the thing about Jubal County is that it is simultaneously ugly and beautiful all at once. There is a rotten core to it, all decaying buildings and pine plantations, but all around those blighted bits are a natural beauty unlike anything you could imagine.

Most folks probably wouldn't see it that way. People are always focusing on the negative and let that blind them to the good there is to see or do. And I think to most folks, that's how they see swamps. They focus on the mud and mosquitos, when instead they could be looking at the moss and the trees.

I also had a couple of things I needed to handle, if I was being honest. Now that I was in the light of day and thinking at least a little more clearly as I'd come down from the deepest part of my high, things made more sense. I was pretty sure that I'd heard that damn redcap roaming around the Camp last night, and I was kicking myself for not having had my wits about me. I could have nipped that little loose thread if I'd had it more together. Of course, tangling with a redcap in the dark isn't perhaps the wisest of moves. But I think I could've handled it.

I'd at least come prepared for it. Sorta.

My mission set, I scooped up my backpack, said my goodbyes to everyone who was up (Johnny not being one of them, the fucking lightweight), and set out into the swamp. I was gonna go slow, take my time, and make the most of it. And hopefully get some shit done.

I waited until I was well out of sight of the Camp before I dug out my weed. The Camp has a real "share and share alike" policy, being hippie sorts, and while I was thankful for a place to rest my head, I wasn't feeling "sharing my weed" thankful just then. So, I found a nice stump that was mostly clean, rolled myself a fatty, and enjoyed the view for a bit.

The morning was a mess of shadows and light as the rising sun fought to cut through the trees that spread overhead. The Spanish moss wasn't as heavy here as I'd expected, but there was still a fair amount hanging down from the limbs above. Light spilling through the gray weave of the moss was a sure enough pretty sight, and it made for pleasant viewing.

There wasn't much of a breeze to stir the air, but it hadn't gotten muggy yet. It had that feel like it would later, but you don't go traipsing around a marsh without expecting to get a little sweat going. For the moment, the bugs hadn't started biting, and that was all I really wanted. Living in a shed with no AC, you learn to deal with heat, but mosquitoes are hell no matter how many times you get bitten.

I was about halfway done with my joint when I saw the eyes peering out at me from around the tree. It was a knotty cypress about forty feet away, right on the edge of a shallow-looking pond. You could see where the waterline usually sat on it, about a foot and half up from the ground, and it was just below that where I spotted them.

Big and golden brown, like a fall leaf turning from yellow to rot, they were probably about the size of an old half dollar coin. Hair like gray Spanish moss framed a small face with pale green skin, the color of the moss growing on that cypress tree. Hell, it was a wonder I saw the thing at all, and if it hadn't moved, I might not have.

I could see it was a pixie, so I gave a little nod in its direction and raised my joint at it. And once it saw that I could see it, it had a bit of a come-apart. It loosed a tiny wail and vanished in the blink of an eye.

Normal folks can't see pixies, not without some serious work. You gotta have power usually, which was why I could spot it. They tended to be kinda shy, though, so I wasn't too surprised when it pulled its disappearing act. I had that effect on people.

They were shy, but they were also helpful and way too curious for their own good, so I knew it would come back in a bit. In fact, it was probably there watching me, and once its invisibility wore off a bit, I would probably see it again. So I just kept on sitting and smoking, taking my time and enjoying the morning.

Those big eyes came peeping out of a fern about a minute later. It was a lot closer now, though still trying to stay somewhat hidden, I reckoned. I could see it had on something orange, which, seeing as pixies usually dress themselves in whatever rags they can find handy, wasn't unheard of. I let it get good and settled, then gave it another nod.

It squealed again, but this time it didn't vanish. Instead it just ducked down low behind that bush. A couple seconds later it tried looking out at me again, from a slightly different spot. I just gave it a little wave with my free hand, and this time it just kept staring.

When I didn't make any sudden movements, it came out from behind the fern. What I saw made my stomach churn. I thought I was gonna be sick. The little bugger had found what I could only guess was one of them flags somewhere, like the ones you roll up in your car window. It had fashioned it into a crude toga-robe deal, which did little to hide most of its green skin.

What horrified me, though, was that it was a flag of the University of Tennessee Volunteers. It was that pale pumpkin-puke orange that just nauseated any true football fan, especially someone who bleeds Crimson such as myself. If you ever see me wearing a turban, then you know that Al Qaeda must be playing Tennessee this week.

I know that pixie didn't know no better, but damn, it wasn't a good look. It was always weird as hell seeing creatures of myth and legend mixed up in modern-day crap, but this took the cake. I couldn't fix much wrong with this world, but I'd be damned if I let this affront to nature go unchecked.

Digging around in my backpack, I pulled out the spare shirt I'd packed. I'm not usually one to worry about fresh clothes, mind you, but Krista wouldn't let me get back in her car if I was too muddy. But this was too important, so I whipped out this delightful little sleeveless number I had, complete with a much-faded Dale Earnhardt grinning on the front. I also scooped up a fairly crushed pack of Zebra Cakes and crammed one into my mouth.

Looking closer, I could see that the plastic bottle of rotgut whiskey at the bottom of my pack only had about three sips left in it. I pulled that out, too, and took a good pull on it, leaving just a little bit there in the bottom. It burned my throat, seeing as it was raw from having been the site of some fairly violent vomiting not thirty minutes or so earlier, but I figured the whiskey might help settle my stomach a bit.

Getting up from the stump, I placed the shirt where I'd just been sitting and then placed the other Zebra cake on top. I took the cap from the whiskey bottle and placed it gently beside, then tried to pour the remains of the liquor into it without spilling too much on the shirt. There wasn't a whole lot to spill, really, and when I was done I had a mostly full cap.

Slowly walking back, I made waving motions toward the treasure pile. That big-eyed pixie just stared for a bit, watching me more than paying attention to the goodies I had left behind. But after I was far enough away, it started matching me step for step, gradually getting closer. I got tired of walking, but by that point it had clearly caught a scent of the liquor. It didn't bother paying me no never-mind anymore.

A foot of green-skinned magic became a blur as it lunged for the cap. It was more than a shot glass in its hands, but it pounded it back just like I would have a shot of tequila from a bar. It didn't care that it was bottom-shelf booze; you'd have thought it was mana from on high the way its face got all blissful. It loosed a little hiccup as it tossed the cap to one side.

Pixies love booze, but can't handle it. At all.

Its skin began to shift in colors. It faded from green to brown, then took on a purple hue. From that it went to red, and after a second, blue. Pixies are also natural chameleons, and when they drink, that color shifting goes on the fritz. It was like a slow-motion tie-dye shirt.

Then it went for the Zebra Cake. Damn, thing unhinged its jaw like a snake, and even from where I stood I could see the rows of needlelike teeth. Fucking dozens of them, and while I'd never been bitten by one, I'd seen a rat that had been pixie-bit. Not pretty.

It engulfed the cake in one bite, grinding it into a tasty paste among its jagged teeth. When its jaw returned to normal, it was split with a dumb smile, a couple of sprin-kles stuck to its upper lip. Then it flicked a lizard-like tongue across it, and they vanished too. Not that I could judge, seeing as I'd pretty much just done the exact same thing.

The shirt was many, many sizes too large for it, but that didn't stop my new friend from ripping off that hateful orange rag to try and put it on. That shirt had been way too big for me; it had to be an XL at least, so the pixie could have lived inside it, with enough left over to make a week of outfits. If it'd had sleeves, then maybe one sleeve would have been enough, but I like to dress for success. And success means no sleeves.

Its head popped out the neck hole, and then it started bunching up the excess in its tiny arms. This was all hampered by the fact that it was pretty drunk, to the point that as I watched, it got twisted up in the shirt. It tried to step its way free, but that just tripped it up more, sending it lurching off the edge of the stump. It squeaked as it fell, landing headfirst in the muddy soil.

It got to its feet, totally engulfed in the shirt at this point, and started swinging its little fists around. I'd have laughed, but then it opened its mouth and bit a chunk of the shirt out, allowing it to fit its head free once again. It crowed victoriously, a sound more cute than fearsome, then looked over at me.

Those big eyes were almost crossing, but it managed to focus on me for a moment. The little bugger gave a little bow from within that shirt, somehow keeping its footing this time. It blinked a couple times, real slow, looking around to make sure it hadn't missed any more treasures, no doubt. Then, with a loud burp echoing from its oversized mouth, it vanished.

I walked back over and pissed on that goddamn Tennessee flag, putting a bow on my good deed.

It felt real good.

I've Burned My Tongue in Thirst of Peace

Turns out that wasn't the only pixie in the area. As I walked along, I saw at least one other, maybe two. It was hard to tell, as they never got close enough for me to get a good look at more than their large eyes. It had been a long time since I'd seen so many. They were drawn to magic, so Granny's place was crawling with them, or at least her grove was. But I hadn't been there in a few years, thankfully.

Hell, I had one living around me for a time. I named it Jimbo and gave it a nice red bandana I stole from the Shell station in Sumpville. Damn thing made itself at home behind the storage unit and set about trying to keep my place clean. I'd leave out little sips of beer for it—well, I'd leave my mostly empty bottles out is a more accurate statement, I guess. It was actually pretty nice. A pixie is a helpful little thing if you keep it happy.

However, it may come as a shock to you to learn that I did *not* keep mine happy. To be fair, though, it wasn't exactly my fault. Turns out there isn't enough beer in the world to keep a pixie happy enough to keep my train wreck of a shed clean. I hadn't known there was a limit to what they'd put up with, but after one particularly wild night, Jimbo did the equivalent of flipping me the bird and then dipped out. Ain't one come to take its place since.

So yeah, having a couple of supernatural critters in the area of the Camp was somewhat unexpected. But the more I thought on it, the more I figured that they were probably drawn to Johnny's fiddle playing. Everyone with even a hint of magic could tell that boy's music was something special, so I reckoned the pixies felt the same way. That would also explain why the Camp was pretty damn clean, considering a half dozen hippies lived there.

On my nature quest, I came to the edge of a small stream. The little thread of water was just wide enough that I needed to be a little careful jumping across it. If it had rained recently, I suspected it would have overflowed its banks, but for now it just flowed along, a snake of dark brown water. I could see a ways off to my right where it flowed into a small beaver pond, which told me I was heading in the right direction.

My shoes squelched into the muddy ground as I took the leap, but I stuck the landing and kept my footing. There was a small splash behind me, and I felt wetness blossom across the back of my pants. I spun around but I didn't see anything other than some odd ripples in the water. Maybe some mud had come off my shoes as I jumped and caused a splash. *Or maybe there's some sort of water spirit fucking with me.*

That got me thinking of Father Flathead, and my good mood dampened a fraction. There was a reckoning coming there one day, I knew, and I was sure it wasn't going to be pleasant. I thought I smelled a strong fishy smell suddenly, and I prayed it was just my overactive imagination fucking with me.

I scampered away from the creek with a quickness just in case. I was hunting a tree I could climb up in, which wasn't the easiest task in a swamp. So many of the trees were cypress, and they didn't have any limbs even approaching a distance I could reach. Those that weren't tended to be more bushes than actual trees. But I recalled seeing at least a few water oaks and magnolias last time I was out this way, so I just kept at it.

My patience was rewarded after another five minutes or so of not-quite-aimless wandering. I wasn't really sure what kind of tree it was, but it had bark that wasn't totally smooth and limbs low and strong enough to hold my weight. It had some fuck-off big leaves as well, like large oval plates. Each was bigger than my head and had yellowish veins running through them. It looked weird, but it was just what I needed.

Hunching over, I set about clearing off a large circle on the ground. The soil here wasn't too soft; it was less mud and more regular dirt. It was covered with a thin layer of big dead leaves from the weird tree, but they brushed away easily. There wasn't any grass beneath them, and only a couple of small plants. A couple minutes of raking, pulling, and patting later, I had a roughly four foot space totally devoid of anything but smoothly packed dirt.

I dug around in my backpack and pulled out a folded piece of paper. An ornate glyph was drawn on it in Sharpie. I'd been practicing this fucker ever since Krista had showed it to me, and I was pretty sure I could draw it in my sleep at this point. But I also knew just how finicky sigils and such could be, so I wasn't looking to make any mistakes.

With the paper in one hand, I began to duplicate the image in the dirt using a long silver nail that Krista had given me. I was setting out to trap me a redcap, and I wanted to be really sure I did this right. Was trying to trap an actively lethal fae creature for my first ever solo attempt foolish? Yes, very. But, I figured, why start making good choices now?

I'd taken out a redcap before. They burn easy enough, if you can get to them before they can get to you. And I knew that if I left it long enough, that damn thing would end up hurting or killing someone at the Camp. It was probably the mistaken belief that there was a panther roaming the swamp, which was the official story of what had killed Kandra, that kept them from wandering into the little shit's path. And now that I knew for certain that it was around and hadn't wandered off like I hoped, I was of a mind to capture me something a little more rare.

It took me a good ten minutes to get it drawn, as I kept stepping on sections I had already done and then had to redo them, but soon enough I had a scaled-up version of what was on the paper. *Easy peasy.*

Producing the bottle I'd been saving in my bag, I gave it a little shake. It was filled with beef blood, fresh from the dumpster behind the Elk Grove Piggly Wiggly. It was far and away one of the more gross things I'd ever done, gathering up enough blood to mostly fill up an empty water bottle. But now, it was going to pay off. The blood wasn't really liquid anymore, having pretty much just turned to a sticky red goo, but I figured it would work. Carefully, I unscrewed the top and tipped it over into the center of the circle. I somehow managed to not throw up at the scent. It took a good few shakes and squeezes of the bottle, but after a struggle, I was left with a pile of wet red goo in the middle of the sigil, reeking to high heaven of old blood.

The trap was set.

Once I was up the tree a few limbs, I settled in for a wait. The big leaves did a decent job of hiding me, I felt, but I could see down to the circle well enough. Otherwise, it was shady and I could feel the breeze a little bit better up high like this. All in all, it wasn't a terrible place to chill for a bit. Even if the wood was hard on my ass. I pulled out the rest of my spare clothes and tried to turn them into a crude cushion, but really they only took the edge off. I got a boney ass, and padding can only do so much.

I dug out the last thing my backpack contained: the little grimoire I had taken off of Brandt after I'd fucked up his car golem. I'd taken to studying it, trying to expand my spell casting beyond the couple three spells I knew. I felt like I was making progress finally, but even though I'm a reader, this shit was surprisingly dry. You'd think a book of spells would be fascinating as all hell, but this little number read more like a math textbook. And the sigils . . . well, they were on a whole different level. It was like I had laid hands on a graduate-level text for glyphs and hadn't taken any of the prerequisite classes. Which, to be fair, I hadn't. Shit was dense.

You see, a spell only lasts a few seconds, maybe minutes, if cast regular-like, like my little fireballs or my moon spell. One and done. Now a *sigil* was how you got a spell to linger. And while casting a spell was really less about the words and more about the intent, making that spell last through a glyph—well, that was exactly as finicky as flinging a spell was not, if that makes any sense. It only sorta clicked for me, and that was a fairly recent development, and had taken a lot of browbeating from HD and Krista to even get me this far.

And so I sat and tried to read. But mostly, I just enjoyed being in the swamp.

It felt like home.

Throwing Mud Into the Devil's Eyes

E ver have a dream where you're falling, and you wake up before you hit the ground?

I have, and I hate it. Like, it's one of my absolute least favorite dreams. I don't much care for heights, and the sensation of falling is the fucking worst, so that stomach-lurching sensation is a special sort of hell for me.

Ever have that same dream, only you hit the ground in it?

I haven't, but I think it's just because I get too scared. It always wakes me up in a sweat as I sit straight up in bed. I've seen some shit and have had some nightmares, you can rest assured, but nothing scares me awake like a falling dream.

Ever start to have that dream but you are woken up by *actually* hitting the ground?

Yep. I fell out of the fucking tree.

To be totally accurate, I think I woke up about a half second before I smacked into the ground. I have a very faint confused memory of the dirt rapidly closing in on my tumbling form. Think of a brown blur coming toward you at the speed of falling, and that was about the sum of it. Not even enough time to try to throw up an arm or two.

I slammed into the ground, mostly on my right side. My arm was thrust out just enough that I didn't land on it, which was good, or it would probably have broken. Not a lot of milk shoring up my bones these days, if you catch my drift. I wasn't that high up, but had I landed on a root instead of relatively soft dirt, I suspect I'd have been in real bad shape.

As it was, I had the breath knocked clean out of me. Coupled with the shock of being asleep just a second before—a sleep I hadn't intended to take, mind you—to awaken while falling just put me alllll out of sorts. I was gasping like a fish out of water, just trying to force a bit of air into my startled lungs.

That's when I saw just how deep of shit I was in. Because there, a dozen feet away and staring right at me, was the redcap.

It was two feet of pure ugly. The damn thing was gaunt and wiry as a famine victim, with overly large hands that ended in blood-splattered claws. Its head was too big for its body, housing the eyes and mouth of someone much larger. I mean, it was like someone took a toddler and stopped it from growing while simultaneously making it into one of them crazy CrossFit people. Then filed down its teeth.

All that was bad, but what was worse was the fact that since I had seen it last, it had managed to lay hands on a weapon. It had found an old sickle with a cracked wooden handle. The blade was mostly rusted, but I could see where the rust had been scraped off due to having been sharpened.

The sickle was tucked into the rope that it was using as a belt for the moment, as the thing's hands were full with its hat. In both hands it was holding an old-style medieval peasant hat that might have been a different color once but had long been stained with endless shades of red. The darker reds were from fresh blood, such as the new splotches from where the thing was dipping it into the gooey blood I had poured out earlier.

The only thing going in my favor was that it looked as surprised to see me as I was to see it. I mean, it was the whole reason I was here, but I hadn't factored on me falling asleep. The gods were either really smiling at me or, more likely, laughing. So there I am, on the ground just trying to gasp, while the little abomination just looked at me with its jaw a little slack.

Then it slung that sludgy hat back on top of its head, and with a wicked grin it started to pull that sickle from inside the rope belt.

It was inside the trap sigil, but I had to power it up before it could step out—only that was gonna take words, and words required air. I started trying to get to my feet, all while failing to say the words I needed to say. I could at least get my mind working well enough to call up my power, but power without a way to execute it was less than useless.

As I attempted to scrabble to my feet, the redcap started toward me, the sickle raised over its head in one hand. The other hand was reaching for me in anticipation, its blood-stained claws flexing and grasping. And that smile it had—there were way too many teeth to be seen, and as I stared in horror, it ran a black tongue across them. I could see that the teeth were so sharp that they sliced along the length of the tongue as it passed over, thick purple blood welling up on it. If the redcap felt pain, I didn't see any evidence of it.

The grimoire had fallen beside me. It was the closest thing I had to a weapon, so with one hand pushing me to my feet, I used the other to grab it up. I brandished it for a second before realizing how stupid that was. So instead,

I hurled it at the fairy with all the might I could muster while wrong-footed.

Sickle met pages in a sickening ripping sound. My book was sliced cleanly in two, the halves parting around the redcap in a flutter of pages. The fact that an old blade like that had cut slap through a thick hardback book like that with such ease said a lot about what the creature had done to it. And even more about what it was about to do to me.

About the time I got enough breath in me to say the words, the little fucker stepped out of the circle. Because of course he did. Damn thing was breathing heavy, like it was turned on by the thought of killing me, and it started to pick up the pace. For a second I thought about trying to race back up the tree, but I knew there was no way I would make it in time. It would bury that sickle in my calf, at best, or my back more likely. There was only one option.

There was no time to get off a spell other than the one I had already prepared, and that one would do me no good. I only had one chance, one advantage over the redcap, and that was that I was taller—which was rare for me in a fight, so I was going to make the most of it.

I kicked the little shit right in the chest.

That sickle sheared off the end of my shoe, and I mean sliced it right off. If they had been the right size, I'd have lost a toe or two, but thankfully I'd stolen these fresh from the Christian Mission and they were too big. So instead of crippling me, the redcap just ruined my new kicks, and in return took my shoe right in its goddamn chest. Thriftiness pays off.

It yelped as it flew backwards, arms flailing around as it tried to keep its feet on the ground. Instead it landed with a thud, right in the middle of my circle. Before it could even try to get up, I sent the words flying, and the sigil trapped the creature within its magical walls. They shimmered faintly, enough for me to know it had worked.

Ol' boy must have glommed onto that fact instantly, too, because he was *big* mad. He was on his feet and hissing like a wet cat in a second, smacking that sickle into the walls that imprisoned him. They sparked blue with every blow, about as bright as a welding torch, but held firm. It would take something a lot more powerful than a redcap to break out of it, I reckoned.

Now I just had to get the little shit out of there.

Just the Tip

I had time. That sigil would last a good ten minutes or more, Krista had said, maybe longer if I kept feeding power into it. I didn't aim to test that, exactly, but I was damn sure not gonna rush things. I'd already rushed to the ground, and I needed a minute to recover.

Leaning over, I put my hands on my knees and caught my breath. I was hurting a little, but I didn't think anything was broke. I was most worried about my ribs, but after a few deep breaths in I decided that, at worst, they were just bruised. I'd had broken ribs before, and I wasn't there yet. And my shoulder was still intact, so all in all, things had gone to shit but mostly worked out. Progress!

Having caught my breath, I walked over and started to gather up the ruins of the grimoire. That was a pisser. It was mostly in two halves, right down the spine, and more than a few pages had broken loose of the binding in the process, threatening to blow away in the breeze. I reckoned I could fix it with enough time, but putting it back together was going to be a righteous bitch. I ain't exactly crafty in the glue and tape sense, and this was gonna need a lot of both.

The whole time, the redcap was cursing and spitting in my direction, though it had mostly stopped flinging that sickle around. If I ever looked at it enough for it to notice, it would lash out with the blade, so I mostly just ignored it while I got myself sorted. I had to climb back up the tree to snag my backpack, as that, at least, had managed to stay in the tree.

Feet back on the ground, I swapped the ruined book for the jar I had prepped. It wasn't exactly a mason jar. It was yet another prize from the Christian Mission, some sort of fancy glass storage jar, its best feature being that it was free. I'd put a little grave dirt in it, of course. That was pretty much one of the three standard bases besides honey and vinegar. Everything else inside there was sourced locally, as in from inside this very swamp. A bit of Spanish moss for the place, a cicada for the annoyance factor, a couple of acorns from a water oak for strength, that sort of stuff. The real pièce de résistance, though, was a trio of shark teeth, all tied in a line with a bit of twine. That was what was gonna give this spell teeth. Literally.

I unscrewed the lid and eyed the redcap. It took to slamming that sickle into the magical walls, just wailing away at them. I put the lid in between the fingers of the hand holding the jar, then used my free hand to flip the little shit the bird. I didn't know if it was capable of getting more pissed off, but I liked to imagine that it understood what I was doing.

Holding the spell jar in one hand, I pulled the nail from my pocket. I was lucky it hadn't stabbed into my leg when I fell, though I knew I was likely gonna have a skinny little bruise there. Landing on metal is always gonna hurt at least a little, but I would happily trade a bruise over having to pull a nail out of my flesh.

I got right up to the edge of the circle and dropped down on one knee. This put me pretty much at eye level with the creature, and for the first time it stopped. I could see my reflection in its hate-filled eyes, and looking closer, I saw that its body was covered in scars. Some looked recent, but most had faded into a woven mass across its arms and chest. Clearly this little guy had seen some fights. It was a wonder it was still alive from the looks of some of the scars.

Taking a deep breath, I centered myself and called up my magic. I was as ready as I was gonna be, so I flicked the nail across the lines I had drawn earlier, puncturing the ward so I could suck the bastard out and cram him into my jar. Before it could react, I dropped the nail on the ground and sent my magic flowing in its direction. Grabbing the lid in one hand and the holding the jar in the other, I thought I was ready.

It standing there all still and such lulled me, I'm not gonna lie. So I wasn't ready when it lashed out with the blade.

The line I had cut in the ward weakened it but didn't sever the protections fully. It was just enough to allow me to do what I needed, and nothing else—'least that's what I thought. But that sickle hit the weak spot, and the little devil shattered it.

The magical blowback all but blinded me. There was a brilliant blue-white light as the ward collapsed under the attack, a flash like lightning. It was eerily silent, with only the catlike hiss of the redcap audible as it snarled at me. Bright like it was, it was strange for there not to be some sort of boom, blast, or anything at all.

I was already working the spell, and the redcap was already starting to get sucked into the jar. I piled on the power as best I could, as there wasn't time or a chance to even try and work something else. I had to get this thing trapped, or that was it.

It swung at me, sending the blade at my face. I leaned back and thanked my lucky stars it had short arms. As it was I felt the breeze coming off it and heard it whistle as it cut through air. I shouted, and peed a little, but held my ground. On my knee like that, there wasn't any chance of me dashing off, so I just pulled myself back, becoming as small as I could.

It was half the size it had been a moment before, but that rage had come back, and it swung again. The shortness of its arms was now countered by the fact that it was being pulled into the jar, and thus closer to me. It also had no partial wards to slow it down, either, so it was lunging in my direction as it was dragged, using the magical momentum, as it were, to get at me.

Reflexes are a bitch, and same goes for instinct. There is just something about throwing your hand up when something is coming at you, something primal. You can't stop it unless you are thinking about it, and spoiler: I had a lot on my mind in that second.

The sickle was going for my chest, and even though I was trying to lean back far enough that it couldn't get me, it was impossible to tell in the moment if I had gotten out of range. And so the hand holding the jar lid flicked up, my lizard brain deciding that the lid would be a better shield than my sternum.

The blade sliced off the tip of my finger. Right fucking off, down to the bone, a bit of my fingernail going with it. I shrieked bloody murder as I watched the end of my favorite finger leave my body, my coke nail joining it. Pain like I couldn't imagine raced up my arm, and I stared with dumb horror as blood began to flow down my finger.

It was almost in the jar, but I swear I heard that little fuck laughing insanely. It was still just a swinging that sickle, but it was too small to reach me now, not that I was totally focused on that fact. I was mostly losing my mind that I was down a fingertip, and not a small section of it, either. Somehow, I struggled through the pain and kept the power bearing down on the redcap, jamming him into the jar.

Even though it wasn't totally shrunk down, it was close enough, so I hit it with the lid a few times as it was sucked in. That shut it up. Literally.

I sealed the jar, barely managing to hold it together long enough to get it done.

Dropping the jar, I grabbed my wounded appendage around the wrist with my other hand, looking close at the bloody nub of my ring finger.

Then I passed the fuck out.

Carry On, My Wayward Son

I was probably only out for a few seconds. I mean, nothing seemed all that different: I was still bleeding, the redcap hadn't reappeared, the sun looked like it was in the same spot. I'm no stranger to blacking out, that's for sure, but usually it was self-inflicted. But then the bubble of stress and shock getting popped by your fingertip being turned into a slice of salami will do that to you.

This may come as a real surprise, but I'm not one to carry around a first aid kit. A quick check in my pack found a couple of pretty crumpled up Dairy Queen napkins that were stuck together with leftover BBQ sauce. I'm no health nut, but I figured that wouldn't be the best call to play doctor with—mostly because I was pretty sure I would soak through them instantly, more so than any real hygiene concern.

In the end I wound up pulling off my left sock to act as my Band-Aid. I had a real struggle with it, debating whether it would be better to use the part that had been in the shoe, what with all the sweat and such, or the part that had been above the shoe and had gotten the odd bit of dirt and mud on it. After some wrangling, I settled on just wrapping it up with the top half first, just doing my best to keep the cut up against the inside, away from the worst of the mud.

It hurt like a motherfucker, and it felt dumb as hell to be walking around with a whole-ass sock wrapped around my finger. But when it didn't soak totally through in the first minute, I decided it was for the best. So with one hand, I gathered everything up and put it all back in my pack, taking extra care with my brand new spell jar.

Look, I'm not gonna lie. I was hurting more than a little bit, but that was secondary. Right then, holding that jar, I felt proud. Maybe for the first time in years. This was a thing I had done, a decent magic I had worked, and I was holding the physical product in my hand. It felt like I was actually making headway on my learning for the first time in over a decade. I might have only had on one sock, but I was walking on cloud nine.

It felt . . . *good*. I wasn't used to feeling that way without drugs. I mean, I wasn't, like, fully sober or anything; I tend to be in some form of high at pretty much all times. But right then, I was feeling high on life more than weed and pills. It was a pretty good feeling.

The original plan had called for me to wander over to Morgan's old witch house to see if she'd left anything useful behind, but with recent developments, I decided that could wait until tomorrow. For now I wanted to head on back to the Camp and see if they had something better than a sock for me to put on my slice. I figured a few beers, a little jazz from my box of oblivion, and some time spent amongst all them hippy fucks would be just the cherry to put on this day.

I spotted a crow in a tree nearby, and even that didn't manage to harsh my mellow. I knew Granny liked to use them as spies, so I did my usual and chucked a few sticks in its direction on the off chance it was one of hers. But the odds of that were slim, and even if it was, to hell with it. Couldn't no one get me down now! I had too much happy flowing through my veins.

With a smile on my face I headed back to the Camp, humming some nameless tune.

"I think that does it," Emily said, gathering up the bits of trash left from her doctoring of my wound.

I held my hand up and took a look. Sure enough, my finger was wrapped up nice and tight. It was throbbing, but I had stuff for that. Mostly I just needed it wrapped up in something cleaner than a sock, and Emily had been nice enough to get out the Camp first aid kit and play at being a nurse for a bit. "Thanks," I said, giving her a nice big smile.

She just nodded, matching my smile. I was certain she hadn't believed the bullshit story I cooked up about tripping on a log, but she was the kind of nice that didn't press me about it. Emily had a way of taking things as they were but seeing them in the best light, if that makes sense. Just being around her could make a body feel decent about themselves, and mixed with how good I was feeling about myself already . . . well, it felt plain nice.

It was moving on toward later afternoon, and the Camp was almost empty. Emily was the only other person around, everyone else having left for the day while I had been out. Even Johnny was gone, off on a supply run, as it turned out. There was some sort of to-do going on that night, but I hadn't bothered to pay too much attention. Someone was leaving, maybe? *Is it a going away party?*

Whatever was going on, it meant I had an hour or two to relax before folks started showing back up, according to Emily, and damned if there wasn't a hammock calling my name. I figured I might could even catch a little nap before things kicked off if I played my cards right and took the right cocktail.

Eyes on the prize, I got to my feet of a mind to head for the hammock and do a quick run as a pharmacist. I was in the midst of a big back-popping stretch when Emily spoke up again.

"You ever think about coming to stay out here, Howard? For more than just a visit?" She was leaned up against the corner of the camper that she and Johnny called home. The sun was behind her a bit, and it sorta shone a little through the pale gold sundress she was wearing. Just enough to hint at the outline of her body within, casting her blonde hair in a bit of a halo. She looked a bit like an angel, I thought, and for a moment I think I fell just a little in love with her. Not for real like, but I hope you know sorta what I mean.

Looking away, I just laughed. I hoped I wasn't blushing. "Hell, you don't need that kind of trouble. I'm best off in my shed where I can't bother nobody."

"You're too hard on yourself," she said. "We have the room, especially now that a few folks have moved off, and it would get you out away from the city. Away from the cops. They don't bother us out here. It's not worth the trouble of washing the mud off their cars."

She was speaking my language there, but it wasn't gonna happen. With no car, I couldn't get up to my usual business living out here. Not a lot of copper to be found in a swamp. And weren't too many folks gonna bother to ride all the way out here to hire me for odd jobs, water witching, or finding lost shit. I loved it out here in the swamp, sure, but at this point in my life I loved drugs more, and drugs cost money. And money don't grow on trees, and even if it did, there damn sure wouldn't be no money trees in a Jubal County swamp.

It did make a body feel good to know he was wanted, though. "I appreciate ya. I'll take it under advisement, but I wouldn't go holding my breath," I said with a wink.

She smiled, that same beatific smile that let you know that no matter what, she wasn't judging. "Just please keep it in mind. I talked with Johnny about it after you left, and he agreed. This is your home, whenever you want it to be."

"What, and use up all y'all's Band-Aids?" I said, holding up my bandaged finger.

She laughed a little, then gave her head a little shake. "I won't bother you about it anymore, but just remember, ok?"

"Sure," I agreed, and I meant it. As I walked on back to the hammock, I knew I would think about it. I'd think about it a lot, probably. But I wasn't about to be the little bit of oil in the water of this backwoods paradise, no matter how many leaves I turned over. Some folks just don't deserve nice things, and I already had more than my fair share what with Anna in my life. *No point in being greedy.*

I slipped into the hammock, the limb-filtered sunlight warming me a little. It would have been hot if not for the breeze that was stirring the air, so instead of causing me to sweat, it got me all warm and primed for a nap. Kicking off my shoes, I settled in to do some serious relaxing. I'd basically saved the world not an hour ago, so I'd earned definitely earned the nap I was about to take.

Everything was so fucking perfect. The breeze, the sun, the swaying limbs, the sound of Emily singing to herself as she tidied up the Camp . . . all of it. This place really was heaven, I decided. I was still fantasizing about a life in the swamp as I slipped away to sleep.

Dancing in the Moonlight

I was drunk as hell.

That's what happens when you drink really heavy on not much food. Not that I was really complaining, mind you. Booze don't taste good enough to drink for flavor, at least not at the level of quality I purchase it at, so drinking to get drunk was pretty much always the goal.

The Camp was mostly made up of vegetarians, you see. And while they weren't opposed to making real food if enough company was coming, it seemed I didn't inspire the chef treatment riding solo as I was. Instead, there was a whole lot of rabbit food to nibble on. And me personally, I try not to eat the food that my food eats. That said, it was a pretty impressive little spread, even if there was a bit too much green to be healthy.

They had a picnic table slap covered in pots and plates of food. While most of it looked raw, there were a couple of big bowls of lima beans and purple hulled peas, which were some of the few exceptions to my "no veggie" tendencies. I'd put a real hurtin' on them, too, and I knew that hammock I was borrowing was gonna be the site of a mushroom cloud of bad gas before too much longer. I had no regrets, though, even if they hadn't used bacon grease to season them up a bit.

Turns out it was a bit of a going away party. A woman named Vera, all long legs and blue hair, was moving off to Huntsville. I didn't know her all that well beyond a couple times of sharing a joint around a fire, but she was nice enough. She loved her some politics, and me, I tended to avoid that sorta talk at all cost, so we'd never really clicked. Still, it was sorta sad to see how down everyone else was.

The Camp really was becoming a shadow of itself. When Vera left, there would only be three others besides Johnny and Emily, the three guys who made up the rest of their band basically. I guessed maybe that was why Vera was leaving; she was sorta the odd woman out. Plus, she was trans, and I could only imagine what a nightmare that must be, living in a place like the county.

Jubal County is known for many things: too many dirt roads, poverty, decent enough football, and good hunting. It is *not* known for progressive, forward-thinking folks.

It's a wonder Vera had ever made this place her home at all, and I reckon that says a lot more about the love Johnny and Emily embodied than the hate the county could muster.

So I didn't blame her for leaving, or even really have that much of a personally vested interest in seeing her stay. Only that . . . the Camp was something special, and I didn't want to see it fade away like pretty much everything else good in the county tended to do. Short of moving myself out there, which I knew wasn't an option as much as Emily might say it was, I didn't really see that there was anything I could do to help in that regard. No, all I could do, I had decided, was see about keeping them safe from shit like that redcap.

Though at the same time I had that thought, Johnny was getting out his fiddle, and that sure enough had me second-guessing my resistance to moving out. Fuck, he was good, and I knew that he would work his own sort of magic and bring up the mood in the room a bit. That man was a wizard of the strings, which I was pretty sure was a lot more useful than a wizard of the drugs such as myself.

I was about to settle in to watch, pour myself another big glass of Jack and Coke from the stash Emily had set out, when my phone dinged. Glancing down, I saw it was Anna, and I don't care what you think, but my heart gave a little flutter. She had that effect on me.

She was just texting to check in. It being a weeknight, we didn't have any plans to see each other, as much as I would have liked that. We only called each other about half the nights we were apart, and even though I was amongst the Camp celebration, my drunk self decided that all I really wanted right then was to hear her voice. So, I got unsteadily to my feet and made my way to the edge of the light, out away from everyone. I didn't want to be trying to talk over Johnny's playing, and I didn't want to be a distraction to nobody.

I put out one hand to steady myself against one of the trees my hammock was attached to and decided to rock a quick piss. I was breaking the seal, but it was coming sooner or later, and I figured why not let it flow before I settled in? That way I would have both hands if I needed them, which seemed really important to drunk me.

Back behind me, in the center of it all, the sound of a fiddle started up. It was promptly joined by an acoustic guitar as one of Johnny's band mates began accompanying. I didn't know what song it was—I rarely did—but it was peppy. Real high-energy, dancin' sort of music if you were the type. Emily came in a few bars later and started singing, and all in all it was a thing of beauty.

I settled into my hammock sideways, using it more like a chair than a bed, facing out into the darkness of the swamp. There was a faint bit of glow still, what with the fire and lanterns and such lighting up the night behind me, but mostly all I could see was shadow and the looming bulk of trees. There wasn't a hell of a lot of moonlight, just enough that as my eyes began to adjust I could make out the difference between bush and tree, so long as it wasn't too far out.

I sat there a few minutes just listening, enjoying myself as I kicked off with one foot to set me swinging. One song became a second, and as it was turning to a third I worked my phone from my pocket and called Anna. It occurred to me that I hadn't even responded to her text or thought to let her know I was calling. Instead of sorting that out, I just dialed her number.

You know what? Swamps don't get great cell reception.

The call wouldn't go through. I sat there, just sorta trying to will it to connect as I kept hitting Redial every time it would eventually glitch out. I tried sending her a text back, let her know I was tryna give her a call, but it just sorta hung there in limbo.

And you know what? That was fine.

I wanted to talk to her, and I couldn't, and life sometimes is just like that. I wasn't gonna let it ruin my mood. I'm prone to spiraling down, and quick-like. But this time, I wasn't gonna. We were in a good spot as a couple, and I was in a good spot in my mind for once.

It was comfortable there in the hammock, so I just kept sitting, listening to the music play. I stared out into darkness and just sorta basked in the general glow I was feeling. If I turned my head, my vision would blur a bit, like my optic nerves were running on a three second delay or something. So I just sipped my drink, stared, and became a drunken one with the swampy universe.

I wasn't surprised when I saw the first pixie. It wasn't the one I had dressed from earlier, or if it was it had changed into something else, which was unlikely. It was peeking out from behind a tree, and I could see its eyes reflecting the light. Unlike a raccoon or cat, they reflected a pale blue glow.

Raising my glass in its direction, I gave it a little nod. It darted back behind the tree, but within a few seconds it was peeking back around at the Camp once again. And as I watched it was joined by another. Then another.

I'd never seen more than two pixies at a time, so three was out of the ordinary. When I saw the fifth set of eyes, I knew things were getting pretty damn extra. And those were just the ones I could see in my relatively narrow range of vision. No doubt there were others looking in from other sides of the Camp.

I wondered what those in the Camp might have seen, if they would have seen anything at all. Like as not, their mind guided them from looking out much at all. And if they did see something, how quickly did they discount it as fireflies, or the eyes of more normal wildlife? I couldn't remember a time where the true nature of the world hadn't been peeled back for me, so I was left to wonder.

It was so rare that I got to just watch the magic instead of having to do something with it—or to it, like light it on fire. So, I just leaned back and made the most of it. Johnny's magic had created something really special, and intended to enjoy it until I passed the fuck out, which I thought might not be too much longer, especially if I lit the joint I had in my pocket.

I heard laughter from out in the swamp, a strange wheezy sort of laugh that I was certain hadn't come from any-thing natural. I hadn't heard anything like it before, and I wondered for a moment what could make such a sound. But then the band changed songs to something less dancy and more sleepy, and I decided it was time to light up and go to bed. I looked down and saw my text still hadn't gone through, but I decided to try and send a goodnight message, let her know I missed her something fierce. It would go through eventually, I reckoned. But she knew.

She knew.

Zen the Fuck Out

I was humming right along.

And I mean HUMMING. What with being at the Camp, I hadn't fully been able to indulge in my favorite vice to the degree I might usually, which was why I had managed to sleep as much as I had. But by the time I woke up, everyone had once again cleared out of camp. Even Emily was gone.

It had probably been her that left the banana nut muffin on top of my pack, next to a bottle of what looked like homebrewed tea. The muffin had been tasty enough, but I left the tea behind in favor of a mostly full bottle of beer I found sitting on the ground by a chair. It was warm, and flat as hell, but it got the job done.

Being alone meant that I was able to get out my pipe in comfort and imbibe from the comfort of the hammock.

I'd only been there in the Camp a couple days, and it had already gotten me thinking of how I could hang a hammock in my shed. That thing was fast becoming my favorite thing on the planet. Other than the drugs, of course.

I'd woken up, hit the drugs hard, and set out. Total efficiency. HD was gonna be coming to get me tomorrow, so I needed to wrap up my chores while I could. And by "chores," I meant looting the ruins of Morgan's witch house, then burying this spell jar somewhere safe so it could protect the Camp while I was gone.

Easy peasy.

The swamp takes on a whole new vibe when you're real high. Add in the fact that this was basically a magic hotspot now thanks to Johnny, even if he didn't realize it, and yeah, things were trippy. I'm not the most grounded of people in the best of times, and being high as hell in a fairly strange place made that even worse.

When I saw pixies, that made sense. I mean, to me. It wouldn't have made sense to anyone not magical unless they were a lot weirder than me. And I'm a weird little shit at the best of times.

But yeah, pixies. I saw them. A lot of them, actually, and more than a few were probably legit. The two I saw bumping tiny little uglies . . . well, I sincerely hoped that was just a drug-fueled hallucination. Because I was pretty sure

I could never unsee that, and pixie dick was a surprisingly horrifying sight.

Beyond the pixies, though, that I'm not so sure of. Like, at one point I swear I saw some sort of six-legged cat-looking thing. Maybe dog sized, it went scuttling across a log away from me, making this weird laughing wheezy sound. Imagine if the Cheshire Cat had been doing the drugs that the Caterpillar was slinging and then looked at itself in the mirror. Only maybe weirder.

It was a lot, is all I'm saying. And not like anything I'd ever seen or heard of before, so that's what made me think it was the drugs. Not that I'm the sumbitchin' Steve Irwin of fantastical creatures, mind you; I just had a fair grasp on the sort of stuff that typically ran through the woods in the county. And whatever the hell that was, wasn't typical.

The whole time I was walking, 'least anytime there wasn't something weirder in sight, I kept thinking about those two pixies banging. I hadn't even known they could. Every damn one I had ever seen was like a Ken doll down below, so just where all those prongs had come from was sure 'nuff a mystery for the ages. I needed some mind bleach.

My mind really was chewing on that, so I guess it isn't all that surprising that I got a little sideways in my navigating. To be fair, a swamp kinda starts looking a bit samey pretty quick. I mean, it ain't like there's that many types of trees and shit to spice things up. Mossy cypress here, mossy cypress there, rinse, repeat.

When I realized my folly, I stopped. The day was young, sure, but getting good and lost would fuck up most all my plans. I knew I had to figure this out, and sooner rather than later. Just how, I wasn't sure, but the way my mind was racing, I was pretty sure something brilliant would come to me.

I took to walking in a circle around this one stump, sorta looking around me I guess in hopes of seeing something familiar. Of course it was all familiar in that it was a swamp, but fuck me if anything stood out. I took to kicking the stump a little, just trying to knock something loose. That's when an idea came to me.

I was pretty sure that I had read that moss only grew on the north side of trees. So, if I could figure that out, I would know which way was north, and that would solve all my problems. I wasn't really sure how just then, but it seemed to make sense. It'd come to me.

Walking over to the closest tree, a knotty cypress growing right on the edge of one of the billion fucking streams in the area, I took to looking. Only fuck what you heard—the damn thing had moss on basically every side. I decided to examine for thickness and such, see if it was growing better on one side over the other.

I slipped and fell in the creek.

Lucky for me, I didn't fall slap in, like on my back or something. No, I just kinda slipped down the short little bank and wound up in water up to my knees. At least that meant my phone was safe, thank the powers that be, but my shoes were drenched. Especially the one with the end of it cut off by that fucking redcap.

I was filled with impotent rage. Didn't stop me from punching the fucking tree, though, even if I pretty much instantly regretted it. I had, of course, used the hand that was a fingertip light, because I was far beyond thinking. It fucking hurt like the blue blazes, and I just knew it was probably bleeding again. That only made me even more mad, which caused me to sorta thrash around and kick the water, like that was gonna do some fucking good.

That scared the shit out of a turtle, which might have been funny if it hadn't also served to splash water into my face. Swamp water in the mouth did absolutely nothing to cool me down; in fact, it just got me even more riled. I was yelling now, splashing around even harder, just totally having a come-apart as the pain in my hand grew.

I tried to climb up the bank, but taking care and time was far beyond me, so unsurprisingly I made it like half a step before sliding back down. In the process, I rapped the knuckles of my good hand on a root hard enough to skin them up pretty bad. It also served to get the water good and splashed up into my undercarriage. I had literal swamp ass going on now.

I could have incinerated the sun with my anger just then, if it had only been close enough.

A better man would have taken that as a sign to calm down, manage his anger, and maybe Zen the fuck out. But I ain't that guy on a good, sober day, and with more than my fair share of heavy drugs running through my veins, well, it was a lost cause. So, I basically repeated all the above steps, only faster, angrier, and with more shouting.

Five minutes later I was pretty much totally soaked, bleeding from three places, and finally out of the creek. There was probably a turtle dead from fright, too.

My chorin' wasn't off to a great start. But—silver lining here—it wasn't my worst start. Not by a long shot.

Small victories.

Dreams in the Witch House

Is there anything worse than chafing when you are a long walk away from where you can actually try to remedy the situation causing the chafing?

Ok, yes, lots of things. But "lots of things" weren't happening to me. No, I was dealing with a wicked case of chub rub on my thighs where my cut-off jorts had gotten soaked. I'd picked a hell of a day to freeball, not that some equally wet boxers would have done much to help. The crack of my ass was just as wet, and I hated life with a passion. I was getting' rubbed more raw than a dumpster full of Winn-Dixie meat scraps.

My aquatic interlude did wind up lucky in one regard: I was so pissed when I got out that I didn't pay attention to what I was doing and wound up on the wrong bank, which looked slightly more familiar to me for some reason. That made me think that I had probably set out from the Camp in a slightly wrong direction this morning. *Not sure how that could have happened.*

Regardless, I set out in what felt like the right direction. And you know what, other than a maybe two-hour detour to hyper focus on a weird-looking tree limb, I ended up right. Because not long after I managed to tear away from rubbing that branch with my good hand, I found myself pretty much right there at the witch house.

If anything, the briars and thicket surrounding it were even thicker than the last time I had been out this way. And as I looked, I couldn't be sure if the drugs were fucking with me or if there really were that many weird-looking plants. Because there was a riot of color that had me all tripped up mentally.

Every color of the rainbow was there, in its dark bizarro version. Like, it was as if God had asked what colors the plants had been, and he'd only asked a really artistic goth kid. Crimson red blossoms flourished among purple-black leaves, while in other areas there were tendrils of what looked like charred orange blooms spreading from within deep ocean-blue greens.

It was like I had on stained-glass sunglasses, if that makes sense.

I could see the remains of the ruined hut within the brush. After taking another few moments to appreciate just what a sight I had wandered into, I started trying to make my way inside. I recalled getting caught up in some rather gnarly briars last time, so I decided to take my time and go slow. I didn't want to be scratched and chafed more than I already was.

The vines clung to me as I made my way inside the dense wall of colorful plants. But thankfully not with thorns; it was more like they were caressing me, clinging to me like a mournful lover hungry for my touch. I swear that I heard one sigh with pleasure as I passed, which was fucking creepy.

Had the explosion caused some sort of magical toxic waste spill? Were these plants juiced up with the remnants of Morgan's workings? That was my leading theory. That, or I was having a totally extra reaction to the drugs. It was fifty-fifty, but I was leaning to this all being real. Weird, but real.

I came to a stop when I approached to a twisted gnarl of briars. The vines of it were a dark red, like dried blood, with finger-length black tipped thorns. Looking closer, I could see that there was a small corpse trapped within its depths. A mummified pixie was impaled on a dozen or so thorns, as though it had been yanked into the heart of the brush and then drained.

The vines seemed to edge toward me, like they were about to make a grab for me, so I noped right the fuck out of there. I got totally out of the brush and started looking for a better, safer way in. I wasn't about to become magic plant food.

I was really thinking I should just go back and say fuck this place. But on one hand, I was thinking about how if there *was* some sort of magical spillover or something, I needed to handle it in case it was threatening to the Camp. And on the other, I was thinking about how there could very well be something valuable in those ruins, and my greed sealed the deal.

Taking my time, I started to walk around the thickest areas, making sure not to get too close. I thought there might be some sort of game trail through it that I could follow instead of just plowing through like I just had. I mean, I didn't see any more thorns, but I decided to . . . hedge . . . my bets.

God, I'm the best.

Right, so from there I began working my way around, hitching my jorts as I walked in a vain effort to keep the denim from rubbing the hot spots I had developed on my chapped ass. That ship had long sailed, but I had to try. If it got a whole lot worse, I was just gonna drop trow and let the world bask in the sight of my bare ass.

I was about to the opposite side from where I had begun when I saw a break in the worst of the brush. It was pretty wide, wider than most any game trail I had seen, and I wondered if Morgan had been coming back. I'd just assumed she would move on to some place better, but maybe she'd kept coming back, hunting something.

Maybe it was something valuable. And maybe she hadn't found it.

My mind started racing with visions of what it could be. Grimoires, spell jars, and shit I'd only read about in fantasy novels all started to pour into my imagination. I got it in my head that I was pretty much going to come back out of this clearing in a bit as Merlin reborn.

Reaching the gap, I started into it, glad for a space good and wide enough that I wasn't at any risk of touching the bizarre plants that lined the little trail. And if I had been a little less high, I might have wound up proper fucked. But I wasn't a little less high—I was really, really high. That kind of high where your mind races itself into fever dreams and you stare at a fucking tree branch for two hours while you pick at the scabs on your arms with your good fingers.

That same focus zoomed in this big tuft of hair that was clinging to a bright-yellow vine. It was dark brown, and the sight of it tugged at my memory, really tickled my brain space. And since I was pretty sure Morgan wasn't traipsing through the swamp in a fur coat, it meant some sort of critter had left it.

But no critter I knew of made a path this wide if left to its own devices, and most wild things, I thought, would have avoided a site like this. So that meant maybe it was a magical something that made this path. I looked down at the ground to see if I could spot any tracks.

There were hoofprints. Big ones, like if someone had turned loose a one-ton goat. Lots of them, too, making it clear that whoever left them was coming and going pretty regular-like. As though they might have moved in. And that's when my heart almost stopped, because I connected some dots.

Dark-brown fur. Goat tracks. Needed a new home after his last run-in with me.

The King.

Fuck.

Should I Stay or Should I Go

I thought about running then and there.

The King had made it abundantly clear how he felt about me. And if I hadn't managed to suck him away into some other mystical catfishy realm, he'd have pounded me into paste. I'd hoped against hope that he'd stay gone a good long time, but knowing my luck, I really should have known better.

But . . . he wasn't there at the moment. And while I am not a tracker by any stretch of the imagination, I could tell that nothing looked like it had been made in like a day. Maybe. I was really just lying to myself, I reckoned; I had no real clue. But there was loot to be had, and damn, I wanted it. I'd given up the tip of my fucking finger and gotten an almost terminal case of chub rub to be here, and I didn't want to turn tail and run.

I should have, of course. But . . .

I didn't keep arguing. I wanted the things my imagination had told me would be there, and while I was sure I was gonna be disappointed, I could live with disappointment. I am the embodiment of disappointment. What I *couldn't* live with was curiosity. I had to know.

The brush wasn't that thick, so I was through the cut in the shrubs in, like, ten steps. That got me back into the clearing where, not all that long ago, I had been pretty sure bad things were gonna happen to me. Like death. I was already in a weird headspace, what with the drugs, but returning to the scene of the crime such as it was, well . . . it wasn't helping things.

With a lot of the stuff I take, paranoia is a real side effect. Compound that with the potential of a run-in with the King and my history of being actually kidnapped here and it was brewing up a stew of fear. If I let it simmer, I was sure it would blossom into some real terror. Which ain't great, especially when you're blitzed out your fucking gourd.

I could see where the King had made himself some sort of nest-bed thing. He'd found the remains of an old leather couch and piled a bunch of moldy blankets on top. It made for a hell of a trashy throne, and I could smell his stink on it even from a dozen feet away. There were a few bones scattered around as well, but I didn't see anything that looked human.

There was an old lantern sat on the ground beside the couch, the only halfway clean-looking thing in the clearing. I wanted it, but fuck if I was about to rob the King. For all I knew, he had some sort of ward on it that would let him know that someone had grabbed it. Nope, I wasn't that dumb. I wanted it, and bad. But not that bad.

Trying to put all that out of my mind, and mostly failing, I walked over to the ruins of the shack instead. It hadn't been in great shape when I saw it last, what with being exploded by magic, but the swamp had done it no favors, that was for sure. The back wall was mostly intact, though the little window had been blown out and there were scorch marks along its length. But beyond that, there was little to indicate what had been there originally save for a few piles of charred boards and shattered glass.

I suddenly wished I had brought my copper stealing gloves. Because the thought of shifting wood around like this, well, it screamed snakes and spiders. Plus, they would have given a little more protection to my poor finger. But I hadn't brought any, so I just said, "Fuck it," and dove in.

I was not wrong; there were quite a few spiders. But no black widows, no brown recluses, at least not that I saw.

It was mostly big wolf spiders, several close to the size of my hand, which made them some of the biggest I had ever seen. I knew they could jump, too, but thankfully none of them jumped at me, or else I would probably have screamed and ran.

A pile of cracked mason jars was revealed when I lifted up a fragment of what had been a bit of plywood, I think. There had to have been at least a dozen or so, judging from the lids. Whatever had been in them hoodoo-wise was long gone, but there were all sorts of neat little knick-knacks in there that I started to scoop up and put into my pockets.

There was a mummified frog, for one thing. Even if I never used it in a jar, that was going on a shelf of mine somewhere. The pinecones and cotton balls, I didn't bother grabbing, but there were a few small charms and stones that followed the frog into my pants. I didn't know where she'd gotten it, but there was this neat little metal cicada charm, like what would have gone on a necklace. I wondered what she used it for, but it got my mind churning, that was for sure.

At the base of the back wall I found a cross. Like, a Jesus cross—like what would have come out of a church. One arm of it was burned pretty badly, but the actual statue part of Jesus—who was bizarrely muscled up, I thought—was still in one piece. Morgan had painted it up with some sigils I didn't know and added three big silver nails to it, like she'd been the one to nail the Godson on the wood herself. It hadn't a clue what it did, but I slipped it into my pouch, since it was too big for my pockets.

Then a limb fell behind me, and I shrieked like a small child.

I spun around, and of course there was nothing there. But my nerves were frayed as hell, and now I was getting reeeeal twitchy. I needed to get gone, to get safe, before I had a come-apart. But I thought I could hold it together just a bit longer, so long as no more limbs fell.

Lifting up what looked like the remains of a small book-case, that sort of cheap Walmart kind that had mostly turned into wood pulp in the wetness, I found another lit-tle gem. There was a small vial filled with what I guessed were snake bones. There were no sigils that I could see, so it was probably just used to hold the bones, not cast a spell, but it was still cool. I mean, who has a jar of snake bones? Me, now!

This was all junk to Morgan, I was sure, stuff that wasn't worth the trouble to pick up. But to my packrat self, this was treasure of the highest order. If I could figure out any of the sigils, then maybe I'd learn some good stuff. It was exciting, damn it!

I decided that I would look for just a couple more boards' worth, and then I would get the hell out of Dodge. The place wasn't that big, so with that, I had probably taken a pretty good look at the bulk of the space. And maybe I could come back later, once the King was gone. Once he had moved on to some place more interesting.

And that's when it hit me. The King may have wound up here by any number of ways, but sooner or later, he was gonna catch wise to Johnny's playing. And something like that was like catnip to the big satyr. He loved parties and music, and he would go to great lengths to make them happen for his pleasure.

Most humans didn't make it out alive. At least not over the long term.

"Fuck. Fuckfuckfuck!" I shouted, realizing I had to warn them. And hopefully get them to go far enough away for long enough that he would get bored and move on.

Would you listen to a well-known meth head that you'd personally seen trip balls more than a few times? Especially if he came to you shouting about giant goat men out in the woods that would magic you to a debaucherous death if given half a chance? I knew the answer to that, but I also knew I had to try.

I thought about my jar, how I had been planning to use it to keep them safe. It would work on things like pixies and redcaps, the small weird shit. But something like the King would probably just ignore it, or at best it might slow him down. It damn sure wouldn't be enough to really keep them safe.

Slinging my pack onto my back, I said screw it to whatever possible treasures I might be passing up. *My friends are more important.*

And I could just come back, probably.

Giving the ruins one last longing look, I made sure I had grabbed everything. My eyes drifted to the lantern again, but I managed to resist its siren call. I flipped it, and the wonky throne, a one-finger salute, then started from the clearing, moving with a quickness.

And with someone who had any sliver of actual luck other than the bad sort, that would have been the end of that. But this is me, and the fates fucking slow stroke themselves to my misery. So, keeping with tradition, I had made it maybe a score of yards when I heard the bellow. "MAAAARSH!"

Kiss My Ashes Goodbye

I ran. I ain't ashamed to say it. I ran and I screamed.

My thighs were on fire, and I didn't care. I'd trade a lifetime of chub rub for actually getting to have a lifetime that was longer than, say, one minute. Which was my current best-case estimate.

Mustering all the courage I had in me, I risked a look behind me.

There he was—the King, in all his bulbous, rancid glory. Far taller than me, and easily four or five times as broad, his body was just slabs of fat hung on a frame that hinted at a tremendous amount of muscle. And mad? Son, he was fucking frothing at the mouth, he was so pissed. His eyes were bloodshot and actually glowing red a little, which wudn't a good sign. He was really just bellowing sounds instead of words behind me, the anger having overpowered his ability to speak.

In one hand he was clutching onto what looked like an old cane pole, like what us poor folks used for fishing. It was comically small, far too tiny to be supporting his bulk, but somehow he was leaning hard on it as he lumbered behind me, and it wasn't even bowing slightly. To me that said magic was at work, which probably wasn't to my advantage. I saw, though, that his right leg, the one the pole was supporting, had a scarred, withered look to it. The hair had mostly fallen from it, revealing a mass of purpling scars that looked like a shark bite more than anything.

And that was what was saving me. He was looking fuckin' rough, and limping pretty badly. Clearly his run-in with Flathead had messed him up something fierce, and he'd gotten roughed up bad enough that even his magically boosted healing hadn't been able to keep up. That was the only reason he hadn't hawked me down, but he was gaining on me, though not real fast.

It was fast enough that he would catch me, though. There was no getting around that. I had to buy time, see what bullshit I could come up with. And even though there was no chance I lived through this, maybe I could hurt him enough that he might go somewhere else and leave my friends alone.

Turning abruptly, I decided that he probably couldn't corner all that well. Well, I was more praying that was the case than actually seeing any real evidence of that as I hooked a hard left. I wanted to get all that magic-infused brush between me and the King in hopes of gaining some seconds. Maybe it would slow him, maybe it wouldn't, but it beat running across the open.

I started calling up my power. The only thing going for me was the fact I was full to the brim with drugs, and I planned to burn through every last drop of them hurling magic at the fat fuck. Every hair on my body began to crackle with energy, and I would have bet my bottom dollar that tubby's eyes weren't the only ones glowing just then.

The King didn't bother slowing, instead plowing right into the brush, which was about what I'd expected. That was it, though; that was all I could do. There was no more time to run. I just had about twenty seconds, if I was lucky, to put a hurting on this guy before he squashed me like a bug.

I hit a knee and slung my pack off as I started to fish for my jar. I didn't know what would happen if I chucked it at the King, but I intended to find out. Rough plan formulated, I was suddenly deflated as I realized I couldn't work the fucking zipper. It got stuck, like, two seconds in, caught up on one of the cloth lips. I took to snatching at it as I glanced up.

The King hadn't bothered finding his trail in; he was making a new one in the magical hedge. I could see that it had slowed him by maybe a slight fraction of a second, maybe, but really, what can bushes do to a ton of angry goat man? They might as well have been one of those big paper banners that sports teams run through.

I broke the zipper finally in such a way that I was able to just pull the mouth of my backpack open. This was all made that much more difficult by my buggered up finger, but to be fair I couldn't devote a lot of headspace to my finger when the rest of my body was about to join my missing tip. And of course the jar, which had been nestled nicely on top of all my shit, was now burrowed down amongst the random crap, meaning I was gonna have to dig for it.

A pained roar got me looking up, and I saw that the King had stepped into some shit. I managed to look right as a brilliant red-gold flash damn near blinded me. The big satyr was wrapped up in some thorns that looked like they were growing to match his bulk. Thorns like knives buried into his skin, and it was only whatever had caused that flash that was saving him from getting gutted. The light seemed to have hit the vines and wilted them enough that he was able to use one hand to pull them wide of his hide. He was swinging that cane pole in the other, hacking around him like a machete.

Eyes trying to blink away the echoes of that bright light that were damn near burned into my retinas, I fished for the jar. Was I cursing? Mayhaps a little. Just enough to peel the paint of a wall, and in a voice that was so high-pitched with abject terror that you'd have thought I had just huffed some helium. But thankfully I felt glass in my hand, and with a triumphant shout I pulled it free from the bag.

The King wasn't totally free, but he was about to be. He was bleeding from about a dozen places, a few thorns still buried in his hide. Considering how pocked he was with spots and pustules, it was hard to tell what was blood and what was pus-laden ichor. Coupled with a withered leg, I stood a chance of actually hurting him, I thought. *Maybe.*

Jar in hand, I started moving toward him. I was calling up every speck of power I had, ready to send it his way, but first I wanted to launch the jar at him, and I knew how my aim could be. I wanted to be close enough that I was sure to hit him, yet far enough that he couldn't just swat me down a second later. So I closed in, pitching arm ready to hurl that mother.

The King hacked away the last of the vines right as I launched it. The jar went sailing through the air, and my heart rose up into my throat when I realized it was gonna smack him dead center. I hadn't had time to pray, but I instantly felt like I owed some higher power a huge favor. Even better was the fact that he was so pissed that he wasn't even paying it any attention; he was entirely focused on me. That cane rod came close to getting hit on his back swing from smacking plants, but it was about a foot wide.

I actually shouted when it hit his chest, an ecstatic cry of victory.

Then it fucking bounced off and fell to the ground at his feet.

Had that been at my shed, I could have dropped it two inches and it would have shattered into a billion pieces. But launch that fucker through the air and into the chest of a rampaging satyr with an anger problem and suddenly decades of industrial glass engineering come to the god-damn rescue. That victory shout wilted like a candle in a crematorium.

I was boned, but I didn't have any more time to waste. It was time to cut loose and go out in a literal blaze of glory. I just hoped I didn't take the swamp down with me.

See, I know, like, four spells, so I'd decided if I was only gonna know so few, I was at least gonna work on those. So, I'd been practicing out at Jimmy's with my fire spell. I kept the worst of the kudzu burned down, and he cut me a little discount on the good stuff. And all the while, I'd been getting better.

Fireballs are great. But fucking streams of fire? Even better.

I pushed my hands together, fingers spread wide, and launched a blast of occult fire right at him. The power rushing through me was orgasmic, and I got to half mast at least as the biggest working of magic I think I'd ever done ripped from my soul and down my arms. A fountain of flame erupted from my hands, sending a beam of licking flame the diameter of a Christmas ham blistering toward him.

The heat of it set me to sweating, and even though the magic of it kept me mostly safe, I could see steam rising up off my wet clothes. I could smell burning hair as the short hairs on the back of my hands charred and wafted away. However, that smell was quickly overwhelmed.

That heat hit the King full blast, and in a heartbeat his fur had caught alight. The stench of it made me retch, and I had to fight to keep control of my spell. It was like mold-eaten carpet seasoned with piss flames and sour milk, like someone was cooking up an omelet with rotten eggs and fungus-riddled burnt bacon.

He roared, and I felt his innate magic pushing back against me. I'd caught his fur on fire, and that would burn good, but I didn't know if any of it was actually hitting his flesh. I needed to be doing real damage, not just setting myself up to wrestle the love child of a fat goat and a hairless cat. So I poured on the juice.

That good feeling was fading fast, quickly replaced with what felt like fire scouring my veins. I was cooking out every bit of drug-fueled magic in me, and it was starting to lash back at me as I stretched my power to the breaking point. I had a choice: pull back and try some other attack maybe, or double down and probably die.

I'd never wanted to live that long anyway.

Burn With That Holy Ghost Fire

I was all ready to end it then and there, but the King had other more vengeful plans. Calling up what I was sure was gonna be enough magic to core me out like an apple, I was all set to call down the fires of heaven and hell on this mythical bastard. But then that cane pole came lashing out from the blast and caught me right across the shoulder.

Being on fire, I reckon, had weakened him a little, because he didn't crush me like a bug with that one blow, although he did send me flying to my left with a broken collarbone at a minimum. I'd broken it enough times to know that feeling, and in a way I had that morbid thought of being glad I was about to die so I didn't have to live with that misery. Then I smacked into the ground hard enough that I worried that I had maybe also snapped a rib or two.

Them magic plants around the King had caught fire, and the smoke they were releasing wasn't natural. I'm talking flames taking on the colors of the rainbow on the tips while the smoke was shades of purple and green. Those bloodred thorns took to popping like gunshots as the fire reached them, including the ones that had buried into the King's flesh.

He was coming toward me, though a lot slower now. He was pounding at the flames that were trying to burn him up, and I could see more of that red-gold glow that had wilted the flowers. Only this time it was bathing his skin, causing pretty much all of him to glow. It was pulsing like a heartbeat, a rapid flutter that I wished with all my might would just stop so he would crisp up into nothing.

Then he stepped on the jar.

It shattered with a pop that was muffled compared to the riot of other sounds, but that sound was like a psalm straight from an angel's sweet mouth to me. It cracked, and there was a little flash of blue light as the sigil flared and died. For a second, there was nothing. I saw that cane rod start to go back for another swing, only now I was just lying there, my head looking like a ripe melon.

But that redcap came boiling up out of the nothing, growing twice as fast as I'd shrunk him down, and he was fucking PISSED. If he knew who he was going up against, he didn't show it. He led with his teeth, his claws right behind, and tore into that bad leg of the King's.

It was hard to see, but I was almost certain that the teeth he had now were not the teeth he'd had when I jabbed him inside that jar. From what I could see they looked far larger and were a dark stonelike color. It was like he had a mouth full of shark teeth—fossilized shark teeth, from prehistoric sharks, only far sharper than any I'd ever dug up.

That cane pole didn't come my way; instead, it went for the little ball of terror burying his face fang-first into the King's shin. I took the chance to get to my feet and call up my power again. I had an idea, but I needed time and power. I hoped the 'Cap would give the former and that I had enough of the later.

The King was wailing on the redcap, who had sunken in like a tick on his knee. Blood and ichor was flying, and that bloody hat was knocked free as the pole cracked down on the thick skull of the fairy. This was my chance—I just had to move fast.

I ripped my bandage off, wincing at the pain, and using the blood that was already flowing I managed to make the crudest of glyphs on my other hand. It was the sloppiest job I had ever done, and it wouldn't work, not like it needed to. But I thought it might blunt things if I could push enough power in at the right time. It would pop, and might crack a few bones in the process . . . but it was a chance.

The King had pulled the redcap free, a fat hunk of his flesh filling the smaller creature's shark tooth-filled mouth. His bellows were equal parts pain and rage now, and as I watched he crumpled to one side. His already weakened leg simply couldn't take it anymore, and it buckled under his bulk. That's when I struck.

He saw me lunge forward and, no doubt knowing I was the bigger threat, he lashed out with the rod, trying to drive me back long enough that he could dispose of the biting shit in his free hand. Not a bad plan, all things considered. And if I was the same guy he'd faced off against last time, it would have worked.

But I wasn't gonna give him that chance.

Pushing power into that wonky glyph on my palm, I caught the cane pole. I didn't time it exactly right—because how could I?—and felt pain explode in my hand as it struck. But I was close enough: that glyph broke from too much magic being jammed into something so flawed and it popped a half second later. Think two almost equal forces smacking into each other at almost the same time and you won't be far off. In short, it saved my hand from getting turned into bone shards.

Even better, it shocked the shit out of the King, and he dropped the rod.

He'd crushed the life out of that little redcap bastard by that point, but it was too late. I took that pole in both hands, and with every swing my collarbone and cut-off fingertip shrieked in pain. And I fed every bit of that anguish into my swings.

And you know what? That red glow faded and faded till it was gone and all that was left was a different sort of red. That's not to say it was all one-sided, 'cause he was certainly trying to get at me and put out the fire in his fur. He got close a time or two, but I smacked his grasping hands away with sickening cracks.

I coulda killed him then and there. If I'd just kept swinging, I'd have swung the life right outa him. And I probably should have.

But I ain't no killer.

That don't mean I didn't enjoy the sheer hell out of smacking some goddamn sense into him finally. Are you familiar with the phrase "getting beat like a rented mule"?

The King is, now.

BACK TO REALITY

I didn't know how the King managed to bow, as bruised and bloodied as he was. One eye was swollen slam shut, and his hide looked mine after Granny had taken a switch to my behind as a child, only on a much larger scale. Where those thorns had dug in and then popped in the heat had left a bunch of thumb-sized holes as well, not to mention the burns. And with that big chunk of flesh missing from his already withered limb, well, it looked like he was on his last leg.

Heh. I slay me.

We were standing there on the very edge of the swamp, up near the road that ran along its length. I was bone weary but desperate to not show it. I had to keep looking strong, because I was quickly learning that the only thing the King respected was strength. Once I'd thrashed him a good one, he'd finally yielded.

And so now here we were. Him, bowing, and me, looking for a trap.

He straightened to his full height, which was well above my own, and spoke with a voice like rumbling thunder in the distance. "Your grandfather and I once fought like that, little Marsh."

"He whup you too?" I asked, genuinely curious. I'd never heard of such a fight, but to be fair, Granddaddy died when I was little and the King and I had never exactly had long conversations.

The King nodded. In a soft crooning voice he added, "It was a fight much like this."

I'd always known the King to have a good bit of crazy to him, but I thought he was having a brief moment of lucidity or something. 'Cause he was not coming off nearly as nutty as any of my other run-ins with him. I decided to get while the getting was good. "Well, you'll have to tell me about it sometime. For now, though, you need to move on iff'n you don't mind, like you promised."

"As promised," he replied, nodding slowly. I expected him to use some fairly loophole I hadn't thought of, but instead he just turned away and started limping away. As he stepped out from the shade of the trees we'd been beneath and out onto the roadside, I could see a little better how banged up he was. It was terrifying that he was still walking. If Flathead hadn't already weakened him . . .

I watched until he was out of sight, then started making my way back toward the Camp. I HURT. Luckily, though, I had recently acquired a cane pole to help me along. And even though I hurt, there is a certain relief that comes with living when you were certain you were going to die.

You know what? Sometimes life ain't that bad after all.

Epilogue

Granny sat in her rocker, easing it back and forth across the porch boards that had already been old when she was a child. The evening breeze began to stir, causing her long gray hair to drift across her vision. With a huff, she began to gather up the loose strands and worked it into a loose braid with fingers gnarled with arthritis.

The sun was starting to fall behind the trees, and shadows were growing steadily longer and deeper around her. If she noticed the mosquitos beginning to flit around her, she didn't show it. Instead her eyes darted across the overgrown backyard, clearly looking for something.

A couple of pixies were dragging a plastic sack across the yard toward the cellar door, tiny muscles straining at the weight. A little bit of blood dripped from the bag, leaving a thin trail of red in their wake. Fat flies sporadically landed on the faded logo of the Piggly Wiggly that smiled up emptily into the darkening sky. They were not what she was seeking, though.

From over the shadowy tree line came a crow, a sleek ebony dart that came to rest on the railing of the porch. It cocked its head to one side, then cawed. It went on like that for about half a minute. As it spoke to her the lines of her face, already locked into a perpetual frown, deepened, and her eyes narrowed. She waved the bird away when it fell silent.

Pulling a snuff can from the pocket of her apron, she took a pinch and placed it on the back of her hand. Two quick snorts later, she felt the nicotine hit and the scent of mint filled her nostrils. It calmed her down a little as she chewed things over in her mind.

Rising to her feet with far too many creaks and pops, old bones protesting being forced to do more than just rest, she began to head for the cellar. She had a few things to get ready before her lesson with Krista tomorrow so as not to scare the girl off. That, and she needed to do some serious thinking about what to do, if anything, about Howard.

Beating the King was . . . troubling. She might have to get more personally involved if things kept on. The thought brought a pained grin to her face, a look that would no doubt have sent her grandson quaking in his boots.

She'd think on it a spell.

THE BACK MATTER!

About the Author

Born and raised in South Alabama, Bob is an author, podcaster, tabletop game designer, and all around hot mess. His cause of death will most likely result from one of the hitchhikers with he picks up reckless abandon. A study in contrasts, he once skinny-dipped at a wedding and is also an Eagle Scout. He has two useless college degrees, has roadied for bands, and broke his wrist in a wall of death at a Divine Heresy show. He's written for video games, designed board games, and owns a disturbing number of roleplaying games. When he was eight he give a camel a coke in Israel and got flashed in Paris. When he grew up he watched a monkey steal a man's wallet in Costa Rica. He's made passible podcasts, filmed terrible short horror movies, and been the producer on a trio of albums you've never heard of. Thriving on the groans of those he has punned around he spends far too much time nervously laughing. He once dug up a dead cow in a creek thinking it was a human cadaver and has a cousin that's a water witch. In college he gave haunted ghost tours (even though he's pretty sure ghosts aren't real). He's been stalked, gave a Prophet a lift, and been stagger drunk in more states than he would care to admit.

Growing up, he was always jealous of the wide variety of jobs his favorite authors listed in their 'about the author' sections, not fully realizing what a hellscape he was lusting after. So to that end Bob has been in no particular order: a warehouse clerk, a roadie for a band, pizza delivery guy, grocery store bag boy, telephone survey giver, inventory manager, quit Walmart after only three days, and currently works in IT. Learn from him sweet children, and flee now to the woods and leave behind the world of men.

More relevant he wrote this book, some other books, and has been published by a number of other folks with questionable judgement. The fictional things he writes sometimes come weirdly true. He lives in the middle of Alabama with his amazing LadyWife, the Kiddo, and a number of increasingly portly cats.

You can learn more at **www.talesbybob.com**

Reviews!

Did you leave a review? In the immortal words of Mathew McConaughey: "It'd be a lot cooler if you did."

Email List!

If you want to keep up with news about my books, this is the best way! I'll never sell or share my email list, and I promise to never bother you more than once a month (unless, like, its super-mega-secret important). To sign up go to my website: **www.talesbybob.com**

Patreon!

If you want even more Bob content, then go check out his Patreon. It's full of short stories, flash fictions, even draft copies of books. Big news also gets announced there before anywhere else, along with sneak peaks of book covers and other behind the scenes content. A popular series on there are 'The Marsh Dispatches' which is an ongoing series of essays written from the perspective of Howard Marsh the Methgician. Check out **www.patreo n.com/talesbybob**

Transparency!

When I started out, I had no other authors that I knew well enough to ask questions about sales numbers, social media growth, etc. I had no idea if my sales numbers were good, bad, or somewhere in-between. But seeing as I'm a big believer in the concept of '*be the change you want to see*' I started sharing all that information in hopes that it would motivate other authors to do the same. And even if they don't, at least this information is available to anyone who wants to know what those types of stats look like for a small time author like myself. So if you visit my website you can see all sorts of behind the scenes information each month, like how my social media grew (or shrank), how sales were, what I tried differently that month, etc. I also break down my stats around my book launches and get into the nitty gritty of each major in person event I do. Check out **www.talesbybob.com/transparency-project**

Education!

I have been helped by countless other creatives and authors along my journey. So anything I can do to pay that help forward, I do. That's why as much as possible I try to keep a host of free resources on my website folks to learn from. If I get paid to teach a workshop, I usually turn it into a youtube video and share the powerpoint I used along with it. If I get asked the same question enough times I will turn it into a blog post or video. I also offer up 'intern' opportunities for folks who want to learn in person sales. And if you want something more in depth, check out my book "Create Your Way to Freedom! How

To Be A Big Success From Someone Who Isn't!" Check out **www.talesbybob.com/education**

Podcasts!

Bob does a lot podcasting. You should go to his website, **www.talesbybob.com** (noticing a theme here?), and check them out. Most of them are related to books in some way, but not all! His best known historically has been Books, Beards, Booze.

Book Clubs!

Want to read this book as part of your book club? Reach out! If you are close enough, I might come speak to it (especially if yall have good snacks). If you are farther away, I might be available to speak to your group remotely. At the bare minimum I will shoot you an email with some bonus content of some sort, and some book club discussion questions. Just us the contact form on my website, **www.talesbybob.com/contact**

About Bearded Bard Inkworks

A real human book publisher, who puts out novels and ttrpgs!

Here at Bearded Bard Inkworks, we are human people, who put out books, and things like books. Booky things. With actual pages. And ink. Except when they're digital of course. Either way, we're absolutely people, and not at all three octopuses pretending to be book publishers. Just look at the top hats. Only a human could be so fashionable.

Look, we love books here at Bearded Bard Inkworks. We do. But we also love rpgs. And general weirdness. So we seek out authors who are exploring unique spaces, while also generating cool tabletop games. Because who doesn't love the idea of finding that next book they love, and then getting to play a game in that world?

Learn more at **www.beardedbardinkworks.com**

STRUGGLING WITH DRUG ADDICTION?

If you or someone you know is struggling with drug addiction and want to get help, then call the number below. It is the Substance Abuse and Mental Health Services Administration help line, a confidential, free, 24-hour-a-day, 365-day-a-year, information service, in English and Spanish, for individuals and family members facing mental and/or substance use disorders. This service provides referrals to local treatment facilities, support groups, and community-based organizations. Callers can also order free publications and other information.

1-800-662-HELP (4357)

For more information you can visit their website here:

www.samhsa.gov/

www.ingramcontent.com/pod-product-compliance
Lightning Source LLC
Chambersburg PA
CBHW061235310726
48971CB00007B/2073